LOVE
IN THE AFTERNOON

ED ZIMMERMANN

The Bobbs-Merrill Company / Indianapolis • New York

THE BOBBS-MERRILL COMPANY, INC.
A SUBSIDIARY OF HOWARD W. SAMS & CO., INC.
PUBLISHERS   INDIANAPOLIS / KANSAS CITY / NEW YORK

DESIGN: HEXAGON INTERNATIONAL

To my wife, Jeannette,
without whom
I could never have written this book

ONE

Whenever an interviewer or somebody asks me, "What made you become an actor?" I get a frog in my throat, and start making little involuntary mouthwash sounds. Then my face goes into a kind of dum dum act. It's not as if I hadn't thought about it. It's just that good answers sound pretentious and the real reasons sound stupid. Anyway I prefer to hear other people explain why I became an actor. This allows me to smile and nod and make challenging little eyebrow moves.

A director friend of mine—a tough man named O'Brian —once confessed to me over a second highball, "Actors are daredevils. I'd never be able to do it." Coming from O'Brian, it was the nicest thing I'd ever heard said about the profession. This wasn't some actor's agent with a lisp and a Cardin suit, or one of those literary ladies with three names who like to talk about art and get their names on patrons' lists—this was O'Brian talking. A guy who'd played lacrosse at Dartmouth, fought in World War II, and went to football games in the snow.

Daredevils! O'Brian was putting actors in with quarterbacks and test pilots and mountain climbers: professions pursued against all better judgment by men who need somehow to find themselves at the center of the dramatic arena. Imagine asking a man why he became a mountain climber? ("Well, my father had this very successful mountain climbing business which he'd built up from a mere pathfinding operation, and I just sort of took it over when the time came.")

Anyway, O'Brian and I have dinner together on occasional Saturdays at a red leather pub on the Eastside called Foley's patronized mostly by ballplayers and minor Mafia figures. On this Saturday O'Brian was in a mood for sports quizzes.

"Who played first base for the Giants in 1944?"

"Phil Weintraub," I answered.

"OK. And the Yankees?"

"Nick Etten."

"Right. How's the wife?"

"Fine."

"You see that guy over at the bar with a nose like a brussels sprout?"

"Yeah."

"Friend of mine. He was a sparring partner for Bobby Ruffin."

"Bobby Ruffin! Remember him against Johnny Greco?"

"Terrific fight," nodded O'Brian. "Pass the rolls." I switched gears to old movies.

"Who directed *King's Row?*"

"You mean with Ronald Reagan and Ann Sheridan?"

"Yeah."

"Sam Wood. How's your TV show?"

"OK."

"How many times were you on this week?"

"Five. Every day. Yesterday was really something!"

"Actors are daredevils. I could never do it."

That was how it slipped out in the middle of all the badinage—like a Croix de Guerre—that sudden little admission of respect! After savoring it for a moment, I lightened the silence.

"Did you know that Sam Wood and your friend with the nose played together on the water polo team at the YMHA?"

"Pass the rolls," said O'Brian.

Daredevils! Believe me, O'Brian is too old and too bald and too rich to throw out unmeant compliments in the middle of a trivia contest. And his description is apt. In or out of work, an actor's life is a study in survival, a primer on living on the edges of extinction.

Take yesterday, for example. I play a doctor on a daytime serial. I wish I could show you a home movie of yesterday at the TV studio.

We pan in on a rehearsal hall at 8 a.m. Those women—opening their eyes with coffee and looking as if they'd just emerged from a bomb shelter? Those are actresses. Later in the day these drained and work-ravaged ladies will swoop and spin into kitchens and living rooms and onto patios and porches—presiding glowingly over their problems, smilingly lovely, exuding confidence and wisdom, speaking endless pages of dialogue (barely committed to memory) as if every word came fresh from the mind and heart.

That palefaced man there, crumbled into his morning paper. That's me, Steven Prince, of the easy quip and the ready smile, muttering now in his daily post-dawn angst about strained back, fatigue, paunch, insomnia, nearsightedness ("Can't see the damn teleprompter anyway, much less read it!")—how will this hero, cast as a TV surgeon, preside in a few hours over a difficult operation ("something terrible in the stomach there")—steely eyed and surehanded, commanding instruments of his nurses in calm, measured tones, cutting here, stitching there, clamping, daubing? I assure you that while he may know things like how many home runs Mel Ott hit in 1943, and how long it took Hemingway to write *A Farewell to Arms,* the poor devil doesn't know a suture from a swizzle stick, and his mind is a panic of instructions and props and terms as foreign to him as the instrument panel of a spaceship.

He's not on until Act III, and for the first two acts (soap operas, gentle reader, are divided into five acts, each roughly five minutes, with about five minutes' worth of commercials, equaling a very rough half hour) he hides out of sight and out of his mind behind the scenery flats, pacing, smoking, running over and over in his mind those evil lines, those cues, those last-minute notes from the director. His hands are pouring sweat into those rotten surgical gloves!

"Act III is the operating room," announces the stage manager. It's hot in the studio (no air conditioning after dress rehearsal because of the noise). An elf is whacking his larynx with a mace and swabbing his throat with road tar.

The red light, and bango! He's on! Oh, with what manly calm he looks into his assistant's eyes.

"Suture."

"Yes, doctor."

"Pulse?"

"Steady."

"Blood pressure?"

"150 over 80."

"Clamp."

(God, will it ever end!)

On and on with those fiendish instruments—sewing, cutting, daubing, talking words, words, words.

"Well, gentlemen . . . that's it." (Closeup of nurse's eyes dilating with awe as he tidies up the wound.) Off goes the red light, the stage manager waves his script, and Prince breathes a sigh of relief that starts somewhere around his ankles and travels up to his sweaty brow.

But the ordeal is not over yet! In the minute of the commercial break, he races in a kind of staggering trot over to another set (his "office"), divesting himself of operating gown, rubber gloves, surgical mask, cap—and falls into the chair.

"We need twenty seconds," hisses the stage manager. (The show is running twenty seconds long, so the director wants the scene played faster to pick up time. Not too serious—unless you worry about things like getting cut off the air in mid-sentence.)

From somewhere a tiny javelin is thrown into his back, lodging in his left kidney. Facing him across the desk is the patient's anxious relative. And boy, is she anxious! It's her first time on live television, and she's looking like one of those frozen swans on a buffet table.

When the red light goes on again, our hero must explain the intricacies of that miserable operation. My God —all those names for things! That staggering procession of terms! Functions! Enlarged thises and collapsed thats and ruptured whatnots! A veritable campus riot is going on inside his head while he assures, calms, places a firm hand over the trembling hand of the trembling relative.

"We'll know more in a few hours."

"Thank you, doctor," whimpers the relative. This man is not a prince in name only! This is a prince for the books! Lancelot! Valiant! You name it! This man is a hero! Look at that jaw!

"Our job," says our prince, beginning a modest smile— but not too wide there, buddy, because the camera is in tight and you're afraid your face may look as if it were coming apart and might fall off and roll under the desk or something.

"Our job," he repeats instinctively, as he can tell by the whites of the relative's eyes that the swan lady has forgotten the curtain line of the scene—something important, too, about when or where something or other—

"We do our job . . . that's all." Inside his head there's a broken record. His exhausted brain can remember only two words in the English language, "our" and "job." The camera, of course, is on him, because the lady's face has gone completely to pieces, and she can't see the teleprompter because her eyes have rolled back up into her head in some terrible way.

Inside his stomach an army of gremlins are swinging baseball bats against his rib cage. Instead of a curtain line he thinks of the director smashing his headset against the wall of the control room, notices that the frozen lady has a button missing on her jacket, remembers how as a kid he broke his arm chasing a fly ball in a softball game— how it cost his father a hundred dollars and how his father kept calling him the "hundred-dollar ball-player."

"The hundred-dollar ball-player can't come to the phone now, he's doing his homework."

"Hundred-dollar ball-player!" he wants to shout at the frozen lady.

Unaccountably, his mind suddenly fills up with lines from the previous act:

"Suture."

"Yes, doctor."

"Pulse?"

"Steady."

His poor brain is playing a tape recording for him of Act III. But this is Act IV, idiot! You're on! Millions of people are waiting! There's an unconscious relative sitting in front of you! The director is screaming! The producer is headed out to the floor with a ray gun! Speak, dummy, speak!

"A doctor just . . . does his job," he hears himself saying again—and gremlins are roasting marshmallows at the base of his skull. He notices that his left hand is trying to crawl off the desk into a drawer.

Finally the stage manager is waving his script at him. The scene is mercifully over somehow, before his head blows up and has to be gathered off the studio floor with a pail and broom.

From what mystic, artesian well strength has come that voice of authority and quiet courage, ready for tomorrow and tomorrow and tomorrow?

Daredevils!

Now look—in the lower left portion of your screen. There he goes—that's me. Watch now as I go lurching out of the studio toward my dressing room like a seasick passenger trying to get to his stateroom in a storm.

Sitting in my dressing room, a towel around my waist, I thought of the joke about the man who, every morning on his way to work, sees a woman hitting her son over the head with a loaf of bread. Finally, after about six months of this, he sees her one morning hitting the boy with a piece of cake.

"Madam," says the man, "why after all these months— why suddenly, why today, a cake?"

"It's his birthday," replies the mother.

Later I stuffed the depleted sack of my body into a corner of a taxi, and, rattling back home from the studio, I wondered how long it would take for the driver to unleash the ferocious garrulousness of the New York cab driver on me. It didn't take long.

"Ain't I seen you someplace?"

"Maybe."

"On the TV! Yeah, that's right. Ain't you on the shows? Ain't you on one of them shows? Lawyer or something?"

There are about fifteen daytime serials with dizzyingly similar names and story lines. And they are populated by enough "lawyers" and "doctors" to start a new country.

"I play a doctor," I said.

"Gotcha! Yeah, that's right. Doctor. My wife watches all them shows."

"Does she?"

"How do you get on them shows?"

Horns screamed behind us. My cabbie cut in and out on cars as if he were driving a Dodgemobile at Palisades Park. But I have tremendous faith in New York cab drivers. I know if anyone gets hurt, it will be the other guy. An enemy driver, his face contorted with rage into the shape of a sweaty bicycle seat, hurled curses at us. But my cabbie didn't miss a beat in the conversation.

"I got a kid wants to be an actor. He's always walkin' around doin' these here imitations—know what I mean?"

"Yeah?"

"Really comical—know what I mean? You oughta hear him imitate Johnny Carson and Ed Sullivan! Really comical! Ya know—like that Sullivan when he says ya know—'really big sheeow!' You know—like that."

A fear-crazed pedestrian caught between a light change held his hand up to us as my cabbie gunned the motor, then threw himself back toward the curb. The cab just roared on and so did the cabbie.

"Once, when we had company, my kid come in with a mask on and a big bag over his shoulder an' lookin' around very sneaky and then run out. Then he come right back dressed like a cop with a big flashlight and he says, 'Anyone here seen a suspicious-lookin' character come in here with a bag over his shoulder?'"

"That's a good one," I said.

"That's my kid. Always imitatin'. Different accents too,

ya know: Jewish, Irish, Italian. I'm Italian myself. See on the shield here, see? Lombardi."

"How are you, Mr. Lombardi?"

I remembered how *my* father would laugh too. The leather mittens that became prize fighters' gloves, the broom handles that were cellos—and I had a hobbyhorse named Winnie who rode with me through the park, across cattle ranches—everywhere. And there were three special teddy bears that my grandmother had made clothes for: Rootsaboots, Joe-Joe Branson, and Sugar. Rootsaboots was crazy, Joe-Joe was a tough guy, and Sugar was a girl. But we'd gone fifteen blocks without winding up under the wheels of a moving van, and I figured it was just as well not having Mr. Lombardi turning around to listen.

"Which side you on?" he asked.

"What? Oh. Right hand side there—in front of the red Volkswagen."

"Gotcha. Is it tough to get on them shows?'

"Sort of."

"Well, nice talkin' to ya."

"Same here, Mr. Lombardi."

I've been on my television show so long now I've almost forgotten what it was like to "get on it." Or what it was like before. Before television. Before the wheel. I *can* remember a nine-thousand-mile one-night-stand cross-country tour in station wagons. There was a bit of dare-devil stuff for you. I can remember climbing out of the car after a six-hundred-mile hop feeling as if I'd left my stom-ach to be overhauled at some gas station two hundred miles behind us, and looking like one of those car crash dummies they use in safety tests. Bent forward like orang-utans we would trundle up to the hotel desk, our faces swollen with rage, and ask for our rooms in strangled tones like netted guppies.

Hotel coffee shops served hamburgers made out of corn-flakes and rubberbands. Twice we were arrested for look-ing like a band of wandering anarchists. And I played *Hamlet* in everything from an improvised gymnasium to

8

a condemned cellar. Five hours of sleep at the Eola Hotel in Memphis on a mattress made out of old hockey pucks, and then hitting the road again at dawn.

And I can remember a particular Broadway drama in which, during previews, the director decided the only possible way to save the show was to "camp" it. This was OK for most of the cast except that I was playing a paraplegic war veteran who tries, in the climactic scene of the play, to lift himself out of his wheelchair and stop his wife from drowning herself. Try getting laughs with that!

But getting back to, or rather on with, the subject of how I got started on television—there was first of all the inevitable audition.

Auditions, gentle reader, are about as popular with actors as getting mugged on the way home from the theater. For one thing, they've had to spend most of their careers just auditioning. People have been known to carp about actors seeming to come on strong a great deal of the time. Well, the truth is, they're auditioning. They can't help it. When, for example, an ingenue asks you for a cigarette at a party, she's auditioning for it. She's giving you a bit of her stuff (smile, wide eyes, voice purring like a catnipped Siamese). She can't help it. It's reflexive. She doesn't just want the cigarette, she wants you to love giving it to her. She wants to say, "This is *your* cigarette. No one else deserves this cigarette."

Or watch an actor walk into Sardi's. Right away he's auditioning for a good table. Not just a pretty good table in the middle somewhere—no, no, table two or three just inside the door—the one next to David Merrick—you know, the man with the moustache frowning at his menu there. The smile, the little joke with Jimmy the maitre d', the heartiness. Oh, God!

In my own case, auditions take on an abstract dimension. I have a hard time believing I'm actually there. The whole experience assumes a surreal quality, as if I'd wandered onto the set of a horror movie while I was really looking for the men's room. The readings for plays in theaters plunged into Stygian darkness as if for an air raid, with one huge naked light bulb hanging over the apron of the stage like some hideous illuminated growth. The wooden chair, the wooden stage manager reading the part of the ingenue opposite you. The whispered asides out front during the reading—unseen faces making faces. Weird!

And auditions for television serials are especially disengaging. All those funny people running around in advertising agencies—guys with beards carrying huge portfolios, puffing up to the bored girl at the desk and asking for Mr. Somebody in Media. What have they got in there? Grass cuttings? Posters from old Jon Hall movies? And all those girls whipping in and out! All the messages, phones ringing, names, faces. You keep waiting for the Marx Brothers to run in and start raising hell!

Readings are held in a big conference room. Seated around a kind of Arthurian table are six men—intelligent, pleasant-faced men. But to the actors they are the Nuremberg jury all wearing blue on blue shirts and looking like they've just eaten an alum sundae. One of them is the executive producer of the serial, another is the producer, and two of them are the client representatives. The client is the man who makes the products that people are reminded to buy on television shows. The man himself isn't there—the chairman of the board or the president. But his emissaries are there for him—are there to be in on the casting of an actor to assume a major role in this TV serial that has been on the air for fifteen years. About twelve million people watch this show every weekday of their lives and it's a pretty big deal. And there are two vice presidents of the advertising agency. The agency handles the account, packages the program, and uses four floors of the skyscraper to run around in. And finally the casting director—young, pretty, with a lot of teeth, a mini skirt, and earth-colored stockings.

"Ready to join the party?" The mini skirt seemed all caught up around her waist.

"You bet," I said.

And suddenly there they were—that phalanx of blue shirts, faces blurred because I had my glasses in my pocket. There were introductions and some general chatter, but without my glasses I don't hear too well either. Jesus, what is that! Swimming into focus was this wrinkled woman half asleep in the corner. Was I dreaming? Was I in the right building? I was eleven years old again. In the reptile house at the Bronx Zoo. Who is that bottled spider in the corner?

It was speaking in a dry, cracked voice—the voice of someone who hasn't spoken for years. What is she saying? (My God, it's my cue!) I thought I must be hallucinating! I started to think of all the places I would have liked to be at that moment: a ferryboat, The Cloisters, Baker Field . . . . But there was the scene to read.

The angry confrontation with my comatose partner over in the corner. I tore into it—accusing, threatening, daring—letting the words fly like a squadron of angry bees:

"I'm walking out of this house, Clara! I came here with a dream of being top—top man and top dog. Not to stay on the bottom with someone who doesn't understand and what's more doesn't care! I'm walking out—out of this life, this town, and this home, which has never been a home, but a *prison!*

(Long pause.)

"A prison!"

The spider lady seemed to have lost her place. Out of the corner of my eye I could see one of the blue-shirted men rolling his eyes and stifling a yawn.

(More silence.)

It was about then that I decided I wasn't there. This wasn't happening. It was a dream. And in about two seconds I would leap over the table and grab that woman by the throat and then I'd wake up and the dream would be over. Only I found that I couldn't leap over the table because I'd lost all feeling in the left side of my body. I wondered if I'd have to drag myself to the door.

"Just a slight stroke. Please don't get up."

The casting director was at my elbow, smiling and offering her arm.

"Sure was nice having you here with us!"

Like a heart patient on his first walk to the solarium, I

11

took her arm and exited to a chorus of pre-symbolic whispers.

Down the elevator and into the street I remembered when I was seventeen I had taken my girl to a football game at Baker Field. And after coming back to her apartment, we'd had a long, sad talk about breaking up and how there just wasn't any sense seeing each other any more. Finally, I left—the girl unforgettably framed in the doorway, tears in her eyes. Halfway down the street I suddenly remembered I'd forgotten my binoculars! So I had to go back. There was the girl, still wet faced and miserable, and I had to say, "Look, I'm terribly sorry, but I forgot my binoculars."

I imagined now having to go back to the forty-sixth floor and asking for my binoculars.

"Gentlemen, I'm sorry, but I believe there is a pair of binoculars there under the table on top of the spider lady."

I walked along Madison Avenue past pipe shops, bookstores, banks, stationers, restaurants, drugstores, hotels. One block on that avenue could service a whole town. Have you ever noticed how people who walk along Madison Avenue wear terrifically concerted expressions on their faces? You wonder if you are too, if you are truly a part of all that grim, frantic hum of concentration. In the middle of all the bustle, a blind man with a tin cup—and a beautiful police dog standing with infinite patience at his feet. It was cold out. The dog was wearing little red booties. I put a quarter in the cup and headed east for Foley's.

A famous Irishman once said, "Every man should have a saloon where he can drink with men he knows away from the cares of home." I think it must have been my grandfather. I'm not sure which he had more of—saloons or friends, but he had a lot of both. And I know he would have liked Foley's. On the wall behind the bar is a photograph of John F. Kennedy and a plaque with the names of all the Irish football championship teams since 1939. The beautiful Irish names: Donegal, Mayo, Galway, Kerry, Kilkenny, Meath. Words like poems. The brave, tough Aran Islanders, and blacksmith's sons from Cork, and blue-eyed, strong-limbed boys from peat mill towns like Ferbane. Heroes!

I remember the first football game I ever saw—taken to the Polo Grounds on a freezing Sunday by my cousin, Bryan McGavin, who had fists like hams and taught me how to stay warm by shoving a newspaper down under my belt into my trousers. Bryan McGavin! There's a name for you!

And God, what a game! The roar of that crowd when Tuffy Leamens spun and tore his way through the Washington team—breaking the field and falling into the end zone with two men on his back! The roar of crowds is like love.

Mike, the gruff-voiced bartender with leg-of-lamb forearms, appeared with a mug of good Harp.

"I see your play closed," said Mike.

"Yeah."

"I heard it was real good," he said.

"How's your mother?" I asked.

"Better, thanks. But it's the *hip*, you know. The hip. But she's gettin' around to the stores now and that. What's up for you?"

"I may do a TV serial."

"You mean one of them soap operas?"

"Yeah. I just read for it today."

"Oh, you'll get it, man! You'll get it. And the women will love you. They'll be proposin' through the mails to ya. 'Dear Steven,' they'll say. 'Oh, Steven, I'm sittin' here and my little tail is that burned up over you! The old man's away so come over for a jug and a round or two on the terrace.'"

"Wait a minute. You don't get it. The show takes place in the South, see. And they want me to play this old wrinkled retainer—an old servant on this plantation in Natchez, Mississippi."

"Colored?"

"Right. He's the son of a slave."

"Oh, I get it. Oh, that's lovely, yes! Go on."

"And he's in love with the mistress of the plantation, Miss Elizabeth."

"I get it. He can't marry her because she's Jewish."

"No. Polish. She's from a very old Polish family in Natchez."

"All right, stop the bull. Oh, my mother will love this! She's a fan, you know—a great fan. What time's it on?"

"I'll know in a few days."

With a promise that I'd let Mike know as soon as I heard anything, I went back into the street again toward home —back into the self-important hum of the crowds and the traffic. Four avenues west was the theater where, two weeks before, people had pulled up in cabs at 8:15 to become my audience. Dark now. Empty theaters are like empty stadiums—ghost ridden.

My wife, Angela, my son, Chris, and I live in a sprawling apartment full of books and paintings, a dog, two cats, a tree, and an aquarium big enough to bathe in along with the sea horses, guppies, goldfish, and assorted underwater urchins.

"How did it go?" asked Angela.

"Great."

"And?"

"And there was a funny woman reading with me with a big bolt in her neck like Rondo Hatten."

"Come on."

"I'm not kidding. She was right out of an old Rosemary LaPlanche movie. She was being fed intravenously during the interview."

"What did they say?"

"She was wearing this broken bat's wing around her neck."

"Do you want to do the show?"

"I might do it for Mike's mother."

"Who's Mike?"

"She has this hip, you know."

"Who?"

"Mike, my friend at Foley's. His mother. She has this terrific hip that keeps popping in and out on her."

"That's terrible."

"Yes, it is. She and that lady I read with today—the one with the bat's wing?"

"Cut it out."

"They were members of the original Celtics, you know. That's where she got her hip."

"I give up."

"Where's Chris?"

"Watching TV."

"When's dinner?"

"The maid got sick. I let her go home. So I haven't thought about dinner yet."

"You were thinking about the maid."

"No, I mean . . . ."

"Get Chris, and we'll go out. There's a new Chinese place I want to try. I'll probably get indigestion and hallucinate in my sleep, but what the hell."

Actors' nightmares are special. They always involve some kind of public disaster. Terrible things happen in front of large numbers of people.

For instance, you're sitting in your dressing room in your shorts, half made up and still madly trying to memorize the third act, and before you know it, you're pushed out on stage in your Fruit of the Looms. Horrendous laughter—like thousands of grotesque figures on top of fun houses letting out that awful, mocking, desperate Hah! Hah! They sneak up on me periodically—especially after Chinese food. I think it's all those kumquats.

I hadn't been off with the sandman more than ten minutes that night before it started. There I was back in the solid glass skyscraper, going back up in one of those elevators with the unstoppable Muzak coming through its pores at you (so you'll hustle out of them faster). God! I'm back to audition again!

Only this time, somehow, when I stepped out of the elevator, I found myself hanging outside the window on the forty-sixth floor like Quasimodo, and dressed in some kind of weird hand-me-down soccer uniform. Waiting out there for my turn to read, and making feeble little taps at the window for the casting director to call me in. The wind was blowing me around and whistling through my shorts, and I was swinging from one hand to the other to keep from joining the traffic forty-six stories down.

Finally the casting director opened the window above my head and suddenly the Nuremberg jury were sitting on the windowsill, kicking at me and rolling their eyes. The wrinkled actress was throwing me cues out the window, but I couldn't remember the lines! Instead I was trying to remember why I was wearing tennis shorts with a soccer shirt.

"I remember now! Some Greek kids stole my soccer shorts!" I yelled up at them, swinging from one hand to the other.

"They swiped it off me in the candystore!" The jury was laughing, and I was thinking if I could just explain about the crazy soccer outfit, they'd stop and let me in to read. But the laughter got louder so I swung around onto a solid glass gargoyle.

(Jesus, what's this!)

The gargoyle turned out to be the spider lady! The one with the voice. And lips like two underdone veal chops. (What is that!) She was trying to hang a kiss on me with those veal chops! I let go—falling . . . falling. . . .

At the point of crashing through the roof of a Greyhound bus, I was tugged awake by my wife.

"You were hallucinating!" she said.

"What! What?"

"Look at your pajamas!"

"Why, are they new?"

"You're soaked through!"

"It was all that goddam lobster Cantonese," I said. "And the kumquats. I should have laid off the kumquats."

About two days after the Quasimodo dream my agent was on the phone. For those people who don't have an agent, let me explain. Agents are people who get ten percent of their actors' salaries for spending ninety percent of their lives on telephones. I'm sure there are other funny things to say about them but I can't think of any, offhand.

"Hi ya, kid," said my agent. He still calls me "kid" because the last time he saw me I was. But we talk on the phone quite a bit.

"Well," he said, "they want you."

"Who?"

"Don't kid around. The TV show, that's who."

He then launched into this sensational narrative about contract, out clauses, salary, guarantee—details hammered out between him and the executive producer of the program in a struggle described in such terms as to suggest the last great encounter between the woolly mammoth and the brontosaurus.

"What about a dresser?" I said.

"A *what!*"

"A dresser. I want a dresser."

"They don't have private dressers on TV serials!"

"I want a Chinese dresser."

"Very funny!"

"A small Chinese girl with kumquats."

"Look, do you know how busy I am! What should I tell them? Yes or no?"

"Who?"

"Listen, what should I tell them?"

"Tell them yes. If they go for the dresser, tell them they can forget about the kumquats."

"I'll give you kumquats!"

TWO

On the first day of most jobs, a man spends the time
looking around, meeting his new colleagues, chatting,
looking over reports, opening and closing his desk drawers,
finding out where the key to the men's room is, and various
other related introductory procedures that help slide him
unobtrusively into the operation with a minimum of
trauma.

This is not the way of it, however, with an actor's first
day on a TV serial. Before actually plunging in, the only
thing he knows is the name of the character he's playing
(in my case: Harlan Cross, a ruthless young surgeon beginning a career at Pinewood Hospital) and roughly what
the relationship of that character is to the story. He's
received his first few scripts about ten days ahead of time,
memorized his lines for the first of them, and tried to form
some idea of the pace and procedure of the day from the
following little schedule that appears in the lower left-
hand corner of each script:

8:00—10:00	Dry for Blocking
8:00—10:00	Makeup and Costume
10:00—10:30	No Fax
10:30—11:00	Camera Conference

11:00—12:00	Fax 1
12:00—1:00	Break
1:00—1:30	Fax 2
1:30—2:00	Break and Film Check
2:00—2:30	Dress
2:30—3:00	Break
3:00—3:30	Air

For me, in whom a simple road map produces blind, unreasoning panic, such a document might as well have been a previously overlooked section of the Dead Sea Scrolls to be teased over by someone with gold-rimmed glasses, pith helmet, beard and pipe. I have spent a lifetime eluding awkward words, arrows, and diagrams—the only kid on my block who never put a model airplane together. Some little man with a German accent and pince-nez glasses would eventually explain "Dry" and "Fax" to me—maybe someday during that 1:30 to 2:00 "Break and Film Check." (Did they all rush out to see a movie for half an hour?) Anyway I figured I'd find out soon enough. Neatly typed on a blue memo sheet was where I was to report:

NETWORK TELEVISION PRODUCTION CENTER
MULTIPURPOSE ROOM 3H—SECOND FLOOR

Ominous. But I'd get there.

The Network Television Production Center takes up a full New York City block and is six stories high. It is a kind of city with corridors instead of streets. A serendipitous complex of offices and sound stages, studios, cafeteria, elevators; units of space connected by hidden stairwells and slave tunnels. Doors with strange words on them suggesting arcane religious cults loom in dizzying succession down endless hallways full of scurrying people who seem, incredibly, to know where they're going.

I stepped warily out of my early morning taxi, clutching my neat memo sheet and feeling a bit like a deserted waif in an amusement park. By asking help and guidance of large and numerous uniformed guards with guns and shoulders like linebackers, I found Multipurpose Room 3H.

"Dry for Blocking" means a first rehearsal (not in the studio) where, with metal chairs indicating furniture and doorways and fireplaces, Max Brand, the director, simulates the setting of each of the five acts. He then gives the actors their moves: when and where they make their entrances, on what lines in the scene they should move here or there, or sit, or open and close a door. In the director's script are written camera shots he plans to take.

"In this scene, camera one will be shooting you, camera two will be on her, and camera three brings the boy into the scene from the other set."

My first impression of Max Brand was of a smallish, wiry man with great energy who didn't walk if he could possibly run and who enjoyed a laugh if there was time for it. That's still my impression. He greeted me smilingly, with no to-do, and bango! I was a member of the company. There's not much to-do time available in that schedule.

The A.D. (director's assistant) copies down the shot plan into *his* script, because later in the control room he will help Max by announcing warnings of approaching shots to the cameramen and the men handling the boom mike on the floor. A production assistant sits timing the scenes and cueing actors as they work through their lines.

Besides the shots and the moves, Max discusses the usual director-to-actor stuff about motivation, emphasis, pace, the meaning and direction of scenes. All of this is, and has to be, done with remarkable quickness, precision, and expertise. A half-hour play is being assembled, learned, rehearsed, and performed all in a single working day. Five of them in a week!

My first day involved my being in three of the five acts, which gave me about twenty pages of the thirty-five or so in a twenty-five-minute script. My first scene was in a hospital corridor, where I was introduced by a colleague to the sister of one of his patients. The second was in the hospital cafeteria, in which I talked to two interns about the first day at the hospital, and the third was at the home of a fellow surgeon and his young wife.

We were put through the scenes with speed, clarity and patience. I was awed by the combination of nonchalance and proficiency of the other actors. In a deceptively stumbling and half-asleep fashion, they seemed to be able to do and remember everything asked of them. They were like a sleepy family gathering for breakfast—each knowing where to sit at table, what cleaning duty was his, and exactly how much time he had to eat his eggs, read his favorite section of the paper, and catch the 8:42, or the school bus, or walk the eight blocks into town. Besides that, they were good. Very good. And nice.

Gustav Reiner, a veteran character man of scores of Warner Brothers epics, offered me the last cherry Danish.

"Please take it. I'm already fat enough. Anyway, it looks terrible. We should take it to the operating room and have it lanced!"

Gustav plays the head of Pinewood Hospital.

"I want you to know we run a tight ship here at Pinewood. No messing around with the nurses. That's *my* job."

"Makeup and Costume," the other item on the 8:00 to 10:00 part of the morning schedule, sprang me loose on another floor which contains dressing rooms, makeup rooms and costume rooms for seven different shows. With some floundering, I found *my* makeup room. But two actors were ahead of me, so I decided to search out my wardrobe lady. There are seven marvelous old wardrobe ladies floating around and mine is named Kate.

"Hello, my name is Prince."

"Oh, Jesus, you're new!"

"Yes, right."

"I'm Kate. Come on."

With a bit of huffing and puffing, Kate found my dressing room and a key to my locker.

"And don't go losin' that key on me! These actors—you can't trust 'em. They leave the keys around and then they blame *me!*"

"I swear I won't lose it. See, look—I'm putting it right on my key chain here—see that?"

"Good, that's the boy. Now here's your doctor's outfit. You'd better try it on."

"Do I have time? I mean, I haven't been made up yet."

"What acts are you in?"

"One, four, and five."

"Well, you better get made up now and come back and try on the costume during Act II."

"What about my civilian clothes for Act V?"

"Wear what you got on—it looks fine."

I started back toward my makeup room.

"Where are you going?" screamed Kate.

"Makeup room."

"Jesus, you're goin' the wrong way! And don't lose that key, for God's sake!"

Ducking back and forth in wrong directions, I must have looked as if I were practicing a curtain call in the round. Gustav Reiner ambled toward me from a telephone booth.

"Confusing, isn't it. Don't worry, I've been on this show five years already and still I'm screwed up. What is happening now, for instance?"

"Makeup," I said.

"Ah, yes, makeup," he said, taking my arm. "We will go in together. Maybe there are girls there."

Presently Carl, the makeup man, was daubing me with 7A Pan-Stik and muttering about my "high complexion."

In the next chair, the hairdresser was putting the final few curlers in an actress's hair, making her look like a diminutive radar station.

"Hello," she said into the mirror at me. "I'm Stephanie."

"Hi, Stephanie. Can you get traffic reports and weather forecasts on that head?" She laughed prettily and made a face. Gustav came up behind her, putting a massive arm around her shoulder and kissing her cheek.

"Stephanie and I are eloping after the performance today," he explained. "So naturally she wants to look her best."

"What acts you in?" Carl asked me.

"One, four, and five."

"OK. I've done your base now and I'll finish you during two."

"But I have to try on my costume during two."

"OK. Come back during three. You better get down to the studio. You've got five minutes."

"Which studio?"

"Thirty-one."

I dashed back into the corridor.

"Kate!" Kate finally loomed around the corner.

"What is it? You lose your key?"

"No, I didn't lose my key, for Christ's sake! How do I get to Studio 31?"

"Go through that stairwell door there, and left down the corridor, then *right* where it says Control Rooms 30 and 31, and down the steps—you'll see these two little steps down. There are some goin' up and through a glass door marked 'Personnel' or some damn thing—don't take those, those go into another building."

(Oh, God!)

Kate obviously wasn't about to take any little caving trip with me to Studio 31; and the men with the guns all seemed to be guarding things, so I set out alone. Down, through, in, out—into and out of a broom closet, clammy with mops and steam pipes. At best my sense of direction is nonexistent. In a trice I was as lost as a baby bat floundering among stalagmites in some prehistoric cavern, groping witlessly through a phantasmagoria of exit signs and arrows pointing everywhere but where I wanted to go. On a deserted stairwell I could hear, very distantly, my name being paged: "On stage, please." What stage? Where? Quasimodo!

I banged through a door and into a huge prop room—acres of chinaware, candelabra, glasses; then out and around a corner where a little sandwich concession lady asked me to get on line. I knew I had to be in the wrong building! The little stairs that went up instead of down!

Behind the concession lady was a guard eating a roast beef sandwich on white bread.

"Excuse me, pal," I croaked. "Studio 31!"

"You in the wrong buildin'!"

"Yeah, right. Look, could you do me a favor?" Somewhere in the right building, my name was being paged—people were waiting!

We started off, kind of half cantering—my guard still eating his sandwich.

"This is really great of you! Thanks a lot. What's your name?"

"Willy."

"Thanks a lot, Willy—I'll never forget you! You ever get around my building?"

"Sometimes."

"Is that my building through there?"

"We're gettin' there."

"This is great, Willy!"

Mumbling my lines to myself and blessing Willy, I got to Studio 31. Court, the stage manager, greeted me amiably.

"We do our No Fax now," he said in a pleasant Southern drawl.

"Right," I nodded brightly. "I had the wrong building there for a minute."

"No sweat," said Court.

The first impression of him as an efficient, sweet-natured man was a correct one. Court's job is to be in charge of "the (studio) floor," responding through a headset to instructions from the director in the control room. Most importantly he "cues" all the action on the floor (signals the actors when to begin, when to knock on doors, when to enter). And in times of crisis, he is captain of fates.

"No Fax" simply means doing the blocking in the sets without cameras. The cameramen watch as the director explains where he's going to want them during the progress of each scene and the kinds of shots he will ask them to take.

A color TV camera, by the way, is a large, heavy, incredibly intricate and cumbersome piece of machinery, and the cameraman must handle it with great deftness. He is responsible for maintaining a visual flow in the action by subtle shiftings of motion, of angle and focus—adjusting to Max's running narrative of instructions, the movement of the actors, and the play of light. The cameras are elaborate machines capable of individually eccentric behavior at times—small, inexplicable misfunctionings that bring a sudden rush of men from the electrician's room like worried surgeons. Like ships, cameras are referred to as female in gender, and so long as they keep functioning to the rigid demands of intensity, clarity and color exactness, they are never turned off—for fear that cooling and then heating the delicate electronic membrane of the machinery might affect them in any one of a thousand small ways. So like mystical sphinxes they keep lonely vigils through the night—glowing, watchful, motionless.

During "camera conference" the actors' use of time depends upon the individual priorities of the given day. If an actor is "heavy" that day—if he is in three or more of the five acts—he will probably find a corner and study. An actress not on until the middle of the show will get some work done on her hair. A small group will gravitate to the most comfortable set (the one with an overstuffed couch) and chat or run lines. Court, the stage manager, had found an actor who wanted to talk about last Sunday's Jets game, and Gustav was holding court for a pretty ingenue, playing an under-five nurse ("under five" is a union term meaning fewer than five lines of dialogue).

"My father was a famous violinist," he explained. "He was constantly practicing. I figured I would be something where I didn't have to do any work. I already knew how to walk and talk, so I figured I'd be an actor."

The other three actors in the hospital corridor set and I took the time to try the moves and business, to adjust to the difference between the actual set and the simulated one in the rehearsal hall, and also to check out the props we were to use.

"Cameras and booms, please," announced Court.

"Fax I" is blocking with the cameras and boom mike— the long microphone suspended on a truck pushed around by one man and manipulated by another who sees to it that the mike is suspended within audibility range over the actors' heads. When the actors move or are separated by more than ordinary space he has to move the mike around, keeping one eye on the actors and one on a studio monitor to see that the mike doesn't get into camera range or cast shadows on the set or across the actors' faces. Inside the control room there is an audio engineer who, along with the video man, the director, and the assistant director communicates through headsets to the boom man, the cameramen and the stage manager: a constant flow of instructions and responses.

"All right, gang," announced Court in his easy drawl, "this is Act I of *La Boheme* by Giacomo Puccini—cameras and booms ready—extras and dancing girls in place— let's have plenty of pepper now, because in September we *may* be going network."

With a wave of his script, he cued the elevator door to be opened by a stagehand. "Lingerie and ladies' wear," whispered the stagehand as I stepped out of the elevator and into the nurses' station. The scene began.

There is a lot of stopping and starting during this rehearsal: camera adjustments, boom problems, line problems. Actors are given yellow tape marks on the floor to mark the exact positions they have to be in for certain difficult shots.

"If he can just give us a beat before he makes the cross," said a cameraman into his headset.

Max's voice interrupted the action over the P.A. system.

"Steven, when you get ready to make that move from the nurses' station to the corridor, take a pause at the counter, look at a report or something—*then* move. Camera one has to pull back there and then pick you up."

"OK."

"On the line, 'Miss McKinley, any report on 302?' "

"Right."

"And plenty of voice there because the boom has to be with the nurse on the phone at the other end of the counter. Court, does he have a mark?"

"Yes."

"Make sure you're on the mark, Steven, because I've got a three-shot on camera two and I have to see the two nurses behind you."

"Right."

Gustav, waiting around for his Act II office scene, interrupted.

"Already he's messing around with the nurses?"

Max answered over the P.A. "I thought you were in the geriatrics ward."

"It's getting too horny in there!"

"I'll get to you in the next act!"

"All right, sweetheart!"

We finished the act and I remembered I had to get back to Kate and Carl during the break before Act IV. Without cherpas or guides I somehow made it out of the studio and back to the dressing room.

"Kate, I haven't lost my key, and I want my costume."

"I got it hanging in your locker." Costume done, I returned to the makeup room.

In the theater, actors do their own makeup. In television, they don't touch it. It is left entirely in the hands of the makeup artist. As Carl worked, I gazed myopically across the gulf between my chair and the mirror, trying to divine some magic transformation in the fuzzied countenance staring back at me. I remembered my first haircut at Best's: how my head felt "drafty" afterwards, and the blue balloon that said "I'm a Good Boy" on it.

In the next chair an actor, his eyes shut, waiting for the ministrations of sponge and pencil, was saying his lines to himself in bleak sotto voce.

"I say, 'But what about Ralph, doesn't he know about Ruth's new attitude?'"

"She says, 'Ralph doesn't care.'"

"I say, 'Doesn't care? How do you know that . . . .'"

Under the hairdryer in the corner sat an actress, doing her nails and complaining about train service to Connecticut. On the phone, the hairdresser was ordering sandwiches.

"Makeup Room. *Makeup Room!* What do ya mean, 'Spell it!'"

On the intercom came Court's easy drawl. "Stand by for Act IV, please."

I sat up. "That's me."

"OK, you're finished," said Carl taking the Kleenex out of my collar. "I'll touch you up again after dress rehearsal."

"Where's my balloon?" I demanded.

"On top of your neck," said Carl.

Fax I over, the actors improvise lunch around the finishing up of details of costume, hair setting and makeup. Lunch! My stomach was still working on that cherry Danish I'd had at 8:15. Some actors went out, some stayed in their rooms, some ate, some didn't. Gustav managed an apple.

"The day here is like some crazy symphony," he said, heading for the men's room with his apple. "Now starts the panic movement." Passing Kate on the way, he gave her a small pinch. "When do we go to Atlantic City together, sweetheart?"

"Crazy!" she murmured, scuttling into the wardrobe room with something needing to be sewn.

The last fifteen minutes of the break are taken up by notes from the director: changes, cuts, advice on playing the scenes, instructions about pace, motivation.

"Fax II" is a run-through. Now the gears begin to fall into place, and things begin happening pretty fast. The casualness of the early part of the day is gone. The mechanics of the operation smooth out and the concentration begins to revolve around the performances. I could feel a new tension come into the actors. They were beginning to dig under the skin of the scenes, freed somewhat from having to think exclusively of technical adjustments: cameras and mikes and floor marks. We were playing the scenes straight through now and the lines were coming thick and fast. The crew had become quiet, intent, as they shifted more fluidly from sequence to sequence, from one to the next of five sets assembled and decorated that morning: a nurses' station and corridor, an office, a cafeteria, a living room, a bedroom.

We still stopped, but much less frequently, for mechanical adjustments, changes, and a sprinkling of line flubs. As the mechanical process of the operation irons out, and the timing becomes more precise, the pressure on the actors increases; the day finally zeroes in on how well you can do all the things that have come to be asked of you in a very short period of time.

A dozen people follow the action in the control room. Max Brand will have notes on acting, lighting, sound, sets, makeup, costume, hair: myriad details poised in his mind to be dealt with and, hopefully, solved.

"Stephanie, my dear, those boots look like something out of a Jacques Cousteau documentary."

"A which?"

"Wear shoes."

In Act IV—the hospital cafeteria scene—I had to appear to the two interns to be a nice, affable sort while allowing the audience to infer that I was really pumping the two men for information and that I was being less than candid with them about myself and my background. In the next act I had to do virtually the same bit with the young colleague and his wife whom I was visiting for dinner.

Max had notes. "We need more variety between the way you deal with the two men and the way you handle the couple. I know it's the same in the writing, but I think you can use the fact that a woman is involved in the second scene more than you're doing now."

"I agree," I said, "but it's tricky, particularly in the fifth act, to make the couple believe me and the audience not, without looking obvious or completely letting the cat out of the bag about the character."

"Try anyway," said Max.

"Will I get a balloon?"

"Two balloons."

Max moved patiently among the actors, the production assistant, Terry, a tall, quiet girl with a whisper voice, at his heels. Terry had written down the notes in the control room as Max barked them out during the previous run-through. Stephanie, the actress playing the young wife, was having her hair fixed while Carl was powdering her face and Kate was trying to get different shoes on her feet. While all this was happening to her Max was telling her there was a half-page cut in her scene in Act II, that she should have more vitality in Act V, and that her Act V dress was wrong. And when she had a minute he wanted her out on the floor to show her a blocking change in the bedroom scene. The girl just sat there nodding. Why wasn't she screaming?

Andy, the lighting designer, wanted to clear up a "shadow problem" in the cafeteria scene. Paul, the costume designer, had another dress for Stephanie; would Max look at it when he had a minute? The audio engineer was talking to the producer about getting a hidden floor mike for the nurses' station. The production assistant was giving a note to Ralph, the organist, about the music during the credit crawl at the end of the program. The hum of voices was like an army of excited locusts voting on whether to descend on a cherry orchard or a pineapple plantation.

Three minutes to dress rehearsal! The day was an ebb and flow of panic. Where an hour ago everything seemed to be falling into place, now there seemed to be threats from everywhere to make the show collapse like a torn truss. I made my fifth trip to the coffee machine, trying to ignore the squad of midgets playing handball in my stomach. Trying out my voice once or twice to see if it would still function, I managed to produce a sound like the distant whine of a dead relative at a seance. Gustav, too, had abandoned his usual insouciant air, and was prowling back and forth saying his lines to himself and gesticulating like a disturbed panda. Court, nibbling on a plastic cigarette, stood in the center of the studio, script raised above his head.

"All right, troops—this is dress rehearsal—we're a little tight on time, so try to keep it moving—and plenty of pepper."

The hum began to die down.

"Thirty seconds."

(A dawn-greeting hush so profound that a cricket chirp would have sounded like the report of an elephant gun.)

Court waved his script, the stagehand opened his elevator door and I was acting.

Thanks to my nearsightedness, I hadn't noticed the addition of teleprompters during Fax II. But this time I became conscious of them: two little boxes that have the actors' lines printed in black letters on yellow paper and held by two men who scurry around trying to keep within lines of vision. The dialogue keeps rolling electrically through the prompters and if an actor "goes up," "dries," in other words forgets, the teleprompter engineer over in the corner of the studio viewing the action on his own private monitor pushes a button and stops the rolling so that the actor can (theoretically) take a frenzied peek and get back into the scene. About the worst thing that can happen to an actor, outside of being put up against a wall and stoned to death, is to "go up." Scenes are timed to matters of seconds, cameras are aimed down the actor's throat close enough to detect a low-grade virus, and he can't move. The precise plotting of every move, every sit, every leg crossing means he's got to stick it out—however strong his impulse to run out of the room or roll under the table.

With the realization that there were teleprompters came the next revelation. I was too nearsighted to read the damn things!

I was at the nurses' station.

"Miss McKinley, any report on 302?"

"Here it is, doctor."

I remembered the note: (Pause, look at the report, move to the corridor.) As I moved, the teleprompter man retreated from me, holding that faceless, whirring blob of a box proudly aloft like Nightingale's lamp—a teasing, mocking reminder of all the times on steaming basketball courts I had felt as if I were looking through the bottom of a Coke bottle.

I got through the act all right, but the thought had been planted: if I went up, if I had to go to that box, I was dead. I imagined two of those large guards with the guns and dark glasses, hustling me out to a waiting van.

The dress rehearsal ended. Court moved to the center of the floor.

"OK. Notes, and we air in half an hour."

Spilling out of the control room came Max, his production assistant with a sheaf of freshly minted notes,

Kate, Carl with his puffs and brushes, the hairdresser, and Hal, our producer, looking worried. We actors gathered in several little knots to run lines with each other for the last time.

The hum again—as of some new and terrible tree-shredding insects, voices, foot shuffling, urgent hissings, swooshes of camera cables, doors clattering, actors talking to themselves, the swish and stir of clothes being adjusted, the pock, pock of powder puffs being banged against sweaty noses. And above the general din, the voice of Max (Prince Hal at Agincourt) exhorting his troops with instructions, corrections, advice.

"In Act I when you ask Nurse McKinley about the progress report I want to change a shot there. So would you go *around* the counter to read it."

"OK."

"And cut the next line about the O.R. and the operating schedule. It'll be a blend from 'Have you seen Dr. Peterson?' to 'I'll be in the lab office if any calls come in.' Got it?"

The girl playing the under-five nurse piped in. "You mean I don't answer him about Dr. Peterson?"

"That's right. Just nod."

"Nod? But I'm supposed to say about how I haven't seen him."

"Well, nod 'no.'"

I tried to smile, but my lips got stuck on my teeth. In seven minutes a red light would go on in Studio 31, and at that instant in time twelve million souls would be joined at the hip electronically: farmers' wives in Topeka, old men alone in tenement rooms, matrons in San Francisco townhouses, drunks in bars, people dying in hospitals or making love in motel rooms—all sharing the exact experience at that instant in time—watching me come out of that elevator and waiting for me to say something to the under-five nurse, and wondering—every one of the twelve million of them wondering—what the girl would answer. Awesome!

I began to wonder what had happened to the actor who had started out with my role. Maybe he just ran out

of the studio one day in the middle of dress rehearsal—
smiling and waving like crazy and running down all those
corridors, through prop rooms, into elevators that go sideways. With Willy after him, probably—a roast beef sandwich in one hand and a big gun in the other.

Max and the production assistant and the whole en-
tourage filed purposefully back into the control room.
Court eyed his clan of minstrels on the floor.

"OK, everybody—one minute to air."

Again the chatter died—and the hush as in a deserted
amusement park, punctuated by scattered throat-clearing
barks.

"Thirty seconds."

Silence. The wave of the script, and I was on—talking,
questioning, answering, doing the cuts and the changes
and the moves. So far, so good.

In Act V it happened. The scene with the husband and
wife. I was doing fine when suddenly I began thinking
about the "more variety" note. Thinking, perhaps for a
split second, about how the scene was playing instead of
bearing down on the playing of it. Bango! I could feel
a tiny hand from somewhere pulling a little shade down
over my brain. I was up! The guy with the box jabbing
his finger toward something that looked like a section of
kitchen wall with a bunch of flies jumping around on it.
Quasimodo! A second is like an hour! The girl, the wife,
the one with the hair curlers and the nice laugh, jumped
in and covered for me, and the scene kept going. (How
does she do it? That sweet little thing with the wrong
shoes and the cuts and the changes! The girl is terrific!)
My mind kept babbling appreciatively as it fought to get
my lines back. (If I get through this I'll send her roses.
And Willy, too! If Willy can ever find his way back to
this building.) Then somehow, out of somewhere, the
words miraculously popped up again in my head like a
message on tickertape. We went on—we finished—it was
over! The girl was hugging me. "Good, good!" she said.

The credits were rolling while Ralph upstairs in his
organ room pounded out the familiar theme music for the
thousandth time. Twelve million people listening together

to Ralph, "Da Da Dum De Da Da De." Probably half
of them humming along with him. Imagine six million
people humming something together!

In my dressing room Max Brand and the producers were
saying nice things to me, Gustav came by with a bear hug,
and Kate scuttled in telling me to be sure to put my
costume in the locker and not to forget my key.

Outside the studio, a small band of teenagers waited
to catch a glimpse of the actors waving goodby to each
other and getting into cabs. I hurried along toward home,
feeling like walking through the cold late-afternoon air.
I stopped by a florist. The day deserved roses. And so did
the wrong-shoe girl. But I'd forgotten her name.

"My darling, you were wonderful!" said Angela.

"Yeah?"

"What was it like? It must have been hard!"

"No, no. Simple. The voices are prerecorded, you know."

"What?"

"Those aren't our voices. We just lip-sync the voices—
so it's really easy."

"Oh, will you stop it!"

"As a matter of fact, that wasn't me. They've got this
guy there who looks just like me. Really amazing."

"Cut it out."

"They just want me there in case this other guy gets
sick or something. Where's Chris?"

"He's staying overnight at Tommy's."

"Let's go out for dinner. There's a new Italian place
that's supposed to have a terrific veal and eggplant dish."

"OK."

"It's called 'veal and eggplant dish.' He's a good actor,
isn't he?"

"Who?"

"The guy who looks like me on the show."

"Very good. And thanks for the roses. They're lovely."

"OK. Get your coat."

THREE

To keep our myths simple is a wish we carry with us
from childhood. And the distinction between good and
evil is the one people want particularly to be surest about.
Hansel and Gretel were clearly good. So were Riding
Hood and the woman who lived in a shoe. Good folk. And
the wolves and witches who chased them and deceived
them and blew down their houses? Bad guys.

Cowboys and Indians, cops and robbers and finally
daytime television serials continue the appealing mythol-
ogy. And now I was a part of it as surely as if I had
stepped dewlapped and mossy-footed from the pages of
the brothers Grimm. I was Harlan Cross, bad guy—come
onto a decent, eternally unsuspecting Midwestern American city, Middletown, where husbands and wives live in
houses and have children who grow up and have children,
and life goes on for them. They are good folk.

The family unit at the center of the life of Middletown
consists of Phil Markham, senior partner of a law office,
his wife, Ruth, their son, Paul, who is a surgeon at Pinewood Hospital, and Paul's wife, Nancy.

Serial bad guys tend to be dark, heavyset, sardonic,
and on the make. They come from other, larger towns
where wise guys live, and they have a low opinion of

women. They are a special breed: ne'er-do-well prodigals, a kind of underworld humanity that now and then surfaces even in the most exemplary of Middletowns.

Having survived my first day on the show, I was immediately faced with a new and different test in the person of Rick Mallory. Rick had been flown in from California for a month or so to play my freewheeling bad guy pal, Dan Ward, a member of the Pinewood staff with whom I was to get involved in various nurse chases and assorted bacchanalian gambols.

Whenever producers in New York have to cast a freewheeling part they immediately think of California, where freewheelers presumably grow like oranges. They are all named Rick or Rock or Troy, and they have terrific teeth and inexhaustible wardrobes.

"Sorry I'm late, fellas!" said Rick on the first morning. Two of the fellas were Stephanie and the production assistant and the other one was me. "My plane was late, and then I couldn't get this chick out of the apartment, and my ex-wife got on the phone. Bad scene! And of course I left my script on the plane, right?" he said, nudging my arm and glistening his teeth at me.

I could see it was going to be a long day.

"I don't know," I said wanly. "*Did* you leave your script on the plane?" Visions of catastrophe danced in my head.

"Guess I better learn the old words, right?" Another nudge, more teeth. And behind all the breeze and banter, incipient panic. The words he was going to magically catch up with during the day were two scenes—twelve pages chock full of difficult and repetitious dialogue—with *me*.

"Do I have a minute to call my agent? I better tell him I made it," said Rick, buck and winging out of the rehearsal hall.

Blessed with twenty-twenty vision and the desperate gall of a cat burglar, Rick spent Fax I, Fax II and the dress rehearsal reading half his lines off the prompter and the other half off bits of paper strewn all over the set—

in drawers, on the desk, in chairs, taped to the telephone. By air time, the set looked as if it had been given a ticker-tape parade up Broadway.

Playing the scenes with him was like watching a drunk looking for his wallet. Ducking his head under the desk, lurching toward the wall where an angry reply to some urgent query had been Scotch-taped to the light switch— his eyes spinning like frightened marbles from me to the prompter and down to the floor in search of his mark, then flying toward another scrap of paper somewhere.

All the time I was trying to be cool, calm, collected Harlan Cross I had to watch my partner flying around me like a baby eagle trying to escape from having its leg tabbed by the game warden. And to try to detect my cues from odd jumbles of words that often emerged sounding like uncoded ship-to-shore messages.

"Now listen, Harlan, this girl has a flat on the other side of town . . . . " came out during the run-through as "Now listen, Harvard, this girl fluted on the town . . . ."

"Tell me about her," I answered gamely, madly fighting off the image of a girl fluting out of town. Rick, meanwhile, was staring fixedly into his right palm as if he were nestling the Hope diamond. His next two lines were written across his hand, the three following ones on a piece of memo paper stashed in his cuff.

Max Brand, the director, was patient during notes.

"You called him 'Harvard' there somewhere."

"No kidding," said Rick showing four hundred teeth. "Hey, funny bit!"

"I kind of liked the girl 'fluting' out of town," I said.

"And what," Max wanted to know, "was all that head movement?"

"Too much, huh?" said Rick soberly. "Well, I see him as a nervous kind of guy, know what I mean? Restless, moving around all the time, never really comfortable in one place."

"I saw that too," I said meeting his eyes.

"But I've got cameras on you," said Max. "I've got to keep you in the frame."

"Roger, check, OK, cool—watch the head—I got ya," said Rick with a breezy wink, doing a little tap dance to the makeup table.

I've forgotten exactly how I survived my weeks with Rick Mallory. Anyway I was too busy with other involvements to do much mulling. Serial bad guys have to keep on the move. What with removing gall bladders by day, stalking nurses at night, and alternately undermining Paul Markham's reputation and gradually seducing his impressionable young wife at odd moments, I was running around from set to set like a fire warden checking for smoke.

Middletown was agog. I was a tireless Rasputin, Bogart in Wonderland. How, the whispers asked, could Harlan Cross appear clear eyed and sure handed at 8 a.m. in the operating room, when just last night Dr. Patterson, returning from a house call at 4 a.m., had seen him bounding out of a roadside tavern with a simpering nurse in tow and roaring off into the night with her in his red MG?

Day after day as the demonic Harlan I chicaned, I charmed, plotted, and schemed. During breaks I would find myself gulping for breath like a long-distance runner resting under a tree. However, except for the fact that I was smoking too much and hardly ever seeing the sun, to say nothing of my family, I was bearing up.

There were, however, occasional cracks in the wall. Like the business of the knee. I have a psychosomatic left knee. I trace it back to when I was fifteen. This big Armenian kid fell on it in a sandlot football game.

"That's some knee, Edna," said my father, scrutinizing the pulsing object. "Offhand I would say that's about a seventy-five-dollar knee."

Dr. Guilbert, our family man, confirmed the estimate. He's still my family doctor, and to this day he insists that the knee was completely cured by him, and that whenever my knee takes it into its head to act up on me, it's all in my mind. "Like asthma."

Among knees, mine is a real award winner in the personality department. Cooperative and personable most of the time, it will suddenly and with little warning go into its act. Out of the blue, it will start walking in a different direction from the one I want to go. Or sometimes it just gets angry and swells; at other times it simply buckles under. Occasionally it gets noisy on me, squeaking and popping like an old radio.

On this day, I was performing a particularly delicate operation on a lymph gland. Eight minutes of cutting, suturing, stitching, and dabbing. During the previous scene in the scrub room, I had felt it start—a popping sound followed by a squeak—as Rick and I washed and then held our hands sterilely aloft while talking about lymph glands.

"Is this your first assist on a lymph gland, doctor?" I said to Rick, my surgeons' hands going into a palsied dance as I felt my knee getting ugly.

"Yes," said Rick as I fell to the floor, my hands still aloft. Rick stared emptily at me, his face a frozen, toothy grin like a mask-of-comedy cuff link. There was no stopping now, we were on the air.

"Slipped on some water there," I ad-libbed gamely, pawing the ground with my right foot like a circus horse thanking its audience. The asthmatic knee headed for the cameraman as I fought with it to get to the door—my mind racing ahead to the operation: images of cutting, stitching, suturing, and dabbing on one leg like a demented flamingo.

"Call maintenance!" I barked, cutting the scene short and hurtling myself at the door.

"Maintenance!" yelled Rick, hopping around and making funny little daubing gestures at the floor with his towel.

"Out here!" I croaked, clinging to the door handle.

"Maintenance!" he repeated, coming at me, his hands still in the air, and grinning maniacally.

During the break for the commercial, I lay in a womblike trance—the couchant lamb before the slaughter; Court, the stage manager, talking to my knee and beating at it out of long-remembered football remedies. Kate, in a grunting frenzy, talcuming my hands and pulling surgical gloves down over them, backwards of course, so that when I was propped up to operate I looked down at hands belonging to Daffy Duck.

Faintingly, on one leg, I proceeded to bark out my instructions backwards, ordering sewing instruments before the incision, clamps before scalpel—all the while fighting my knee to keep it from climbing onto the table with my patient.

Rick, meanwhile, was doing his own frenzied pantomime of pretending to assist—handing instruments back to me after I had returned them, retrieving hardware from the floor, dancing, bobbing, thrusting nameless files, saws, and pincers into my fluttering hands which, however I tried to move them, looked in the wrong-way surgical gloves like ten opposed thumbs.

"Roger, check, got ya," he'd say under his breath, flipping what looked like a letter opener at me and then waiting for me to do something wonderful with it.

Luckily, real nurses are used as nurses for our operations, and they managed somehow—ignoring whatever ludicrous commands I babbled—to grab the right tools from among the welter of hardware that Rick and I tossed back and forth, and force them upon me so that, however crazily, we did keep going and the scene, somehow, ended.

As I collapsed against a prop closet, Rick danced over to me.

"Nice goin', Dad. We really got *that* mother, didn't we? I'll bet there's not a lymph gland left in him!"

Despite the assorted mishaps and occupational hazards, I continued successfully to insinuate the potent presence of Harlan Cross into virtually every previously undefiled nook and cranny of Middletown life. No corner seemed immune to my exotic presence. I was every man's dream of rottenness. It's amazing how natural and freeing it is to play a son of a bitch. The crazy energy of all those thwarted, rotten impulses flowing through you! Ask any actor which he'd rather play: Brutus or Richard III. You'll get your answer before you can finish the question.

"You are going to have all the fun around here, I can see that," said Gustav Reiner, coming into my dressing room after the show. "Here I am, the big Dr. Nevins, head of Pinewood Hospital—sitting alone at night under that gruesome portrait of my dead wife, studying books on viruses and gallstones, and you are out futtering nurses in your MG! I'm out of soap. May I? Ironically there is a shortage of soap here."

"Help yourself," I said, changing out of my operating gown. "I really feel sorry for you good guys!" I said.

"Son of a bitch!" hissed Gustav, lathering his face and producing the look of a pixilated satyr caught in a snowstorm.

"Not really," I replied airily. "I'm just a ruthless and talented young surgeon working my way through Pinewood Hospital."

"Already you're screwing poor Paul. I suppose next it's *me!* Poor old Nevins winds up reading bedtime stories in the goddam geriatrics ward!"

He was right. It *is* fun playing a bad guy. Making trouble is dynamic. It puts you at the center of things. Like Paul Markham's living room with Paul's lovely wife, Nancy:

Act III

Fade In:
Markham's living room: night. About 9 p.m. Harlan moves from the fireplace toward Nancy on the couch. His manner is assured. Hers troubled.

Nancy
Harlan, you frighten me. Did you know that?

Harlan
(*Smiling*) Frighten you?

Nancy
Yes.

Harlan
Why?

Nancy
(*Trying tentatively to express herself*) We've only known each other for a few weeks, haven't we?

Harlan

(*Indicating his drink*) May I?

Nancy

Of course.

Harlan

(*To liquor cabinet. Pours drink*) I've been at Pinewood three weeks and four days, and we've seen each other four times. (*Returning to couch with drink*) This is the fifth. And the nicest. I suppose I should feel guilty.

Nancy

(*Alert*) Oh?

Harlan

I mean, Paul is called away from dinner for an emergency at the hospital, and here I sit in front of his nice warm fire with his beautiful young wife.

Nancy

(*Trying to make light of the compliment, but affected by it*) What every good, charming man should say.

Harlan

(*His voice gently teasing and intimate*) But I don't feel guilty. And I'm not good. Paul is good.

Nancy

(*Quickly*) Yes. Yes he is.

Harlan

(*Wryly*) I'm just a man.

Nancy

(*Feeling his closeness*) I've never known anyone so . . . assured as you are. I think that's what frightens me about you.

Harlan

(*Putting his arm around her*) You're trembling. Should I stoke up the fire?

Nancy

(*Conscious of his arm around her*) No. I . . . I'm fine. Harlan, I . . . .
(*Suddenly he kisses her gently. Struggling with herself not to respond, she turns away*)
Harlan, Please!

Harlan

(*Holding her more tightly now*) You're so lovely. (*Kisses her again, more strongly this time. She responds, then breaks away, moves to the fireplace*)

Nancy

Nothing like this has ever happened to me before. I don't seem to be able to handle my feelings anymore. (*Moved and upset*) I can't let it happen. I'm Paul's wife!

Harlan

(*Seductively*) Sometimes you have to be selfish, Nancy. You have to say "yes" to the feelings that frighten you.

Nancy

(*Visibly shaken*) Please go now, Harlan. Please.

Harlan

All right. (*A beat. He is studying her*) Aren't you going to see me to the door? (*She walks to the door with him. He kisses her again. He turns to go, and we see his smile. He is winning and he knows it*)

And here I am as the ruthless schemer, sowing insidious seeds with Dr. Nevins, head of Pinewood Hospital:

Act V

Fade In:
Dr. Nevins's office. The following morning. Nevins is seated at his desk reading a report. Harlan stands facing him. Nevins's manner is quizzical.

Nevins

Dr. Cross, I see that you have requested someone other than Dr. Paul Markham to second assist you on that trichotomy this afternoon. May I know the reason?

Harlan

(*Pretending to become uneasy*) I didn't expect that to come to your attention, Dr. Nevins.

Nevins

As former chief of surgery, I take a particular interest in anything affecting the surgical service.

Harlan

Dr. Nevins, I'd rather not talk about my reason for the request.

Nevins

Why is that?

Harlan

Because I value the reputation of my colleagues.

Nevins

I'm sure you do.

Harlan

And I know that you have the highest respect for Paul Markham.

Nevins

That's right, I have. Paul is my prize protege.

Harlan

That's why I'd rather not go into it, sir.

Nevins

(*Somewhat impatiently*) Dr. Cross, I have quickly learned to respect your skill and judgment. If you have some reservation concerning any matter to do with the service I want to know what it is.

Harlan

(*After some hesitation*) Well, sir—then I must say frankly that Paul Markham's work has not seemed to me to be up to par in the past couple of weeks.

Nevins

(*Shocked*) Indeed? Would you kindly elaborate?

Harlan

He seems distracted from his work by personal problems of some kind. I've been to his home once or twice recently and he seemed tense and uneasy. I'm frankly concerned about him.

Nevins

(*Disturbed*) I wasn't aware of any of this.

Harlan

I'm afraid I've spoken out of turn.

Nevins

Not at all. I insisted you tell me, and you did. Thank you,

Dr. Cross—that will be all. I will ask Dr. Wilson to second assist you this afternoon. (*Harlan walks to the door, a small smile on his lips*)

Beautiful! All those closing shot smiles and stunned protagonists!

A bad guy, I soon discovered, not only has a lion's share of the scenes, but he's on a lot—three or four acts, three to five times a week. And the sheer size of the audience!

Gustav had dried his face and sat smoking a cigarette musingly.

"Do you realize, Gustav," I said, "we'd have to be in a play for about thirty years to be seen by as many people as see us in a single day on this show!"

"At least by that time I'd know my lines," he said.

Tom Curtis came dragging in, his tee shirt halfway over his head, looking like the rear end of a stage horse in a children's pageant. Tom plays Ian Philips, chief of staff at Pinewood. Eleven years on the show have made him a walking casebook of small and mysterious ailments.

"Is this the bathhouse? I want to wring out a bathing suit," he said, different sections of his body successively collapsing onto my cot.

"How come you have a cot and I don't?" he asked morosely.

"It's in my contract," I said. "But that's nothing. Wait till you see my dresser! She's downstairs now washing out my surgical mask."

"This son of a bitch gets everything," said Tom. "Nurses, wives, cots."

"Why are you mumbling?" I asked.

"I screamed at my kids last night. I can't talk. My voice is gone."

Stephanie popped in, making her second appearance of the day without haircurlers. For most of the day our ladies generally look like illustrations from a book on pillow fighting. But by air time they are magically transformed into fresh and glamorous creatures.

"Stephanie, my sweetheart!" said Gustav coming to vivid life. "Let's have an orgy."

"I've got an appointment," said Stephanie. "I just wanted to find out how Tom's pinched nerve is."

"It's moved down from my shoulder to my coccyx," said Tom soberly.

"Your what?" boomed Gustav. "Something is pinching your coccyx?"

"It's in the back, Gustav," said Stephanie.

"Oh," he said. "It's been so long, I've forgotten."

"Oh, Steven," she said, turning to me with a smile, "I thought our scene went really well, didn't you? Bye. See you tomorrow," and off she went in a cloud of beige and Chanel.

"I suppose," Tom continued, "you'll try to knock Reiner and me off next."

"That's right," I said. "While you suckers are wasting your time on medical journals, I've been brushing up on Machiavelli and *Mein Kampf*."

Cynthia Lewis, our casting director, ducked into the room.

"We're getting a lot of good reaction on you, Steven. Lots of cards and letters!" she said, running off.

"Son of a bitch!" intoned Tom, shielding his eyes from the light with the crook of his arm.

"Eat your heart out!" I said, zapping him with a towel.

And on the outside world, shocks of female recognition in department stores, groceries, and laundromats confirmed my conviction that I had come upon daytime television like Sherman coming into Atlanta. Ladies began edging up to me in Gristede's.

"Aren't you the new doctor on the show?"

"Yes," I'd say, giving it the old modest smile.

"I told my daughter, that *must* be you!"

And the daughters too—looking bright eyed and giggling happily. One in particular, a girl about twenty-four with green, almond-shaped eyes and a terracotta mini skirt.

"I see you every day," she trilled leaning down into the freezer for some broccoli in the stay-fresh pouch. "You're such a baad man!" Southern girl.

"Terrific!" I said.

The image bore in on me of a veritable harem of green-eyed girls in mini skirts reaching into freezers in Duluth and Columbus and Baton Rouge and Memphis—smiling to themselves about Harlan Cross and all that delicious badness!

Oh, they love it! Harlan Cross: brilliant surgeon, demon lover! No poor good guy me! Chuckling and chortling to myself, I floated weightlessly down the street in a private ether of self-satisfaction. A young bull in my bright bass prime—the dynamic center of a constant and raging storm!

Think of them out there, Prince boy—all those pretty daughters with the broccoli and the romaine lettuce, snuggled in front of their little portables, dreaming away about Harlan Cross, as scene upon scene ends with your triumphant, knifelike, bad-guy grin!

None of those nice Mom and Dad scenes for old Harlan, boy! Where Dad says, "I wish you wouldn't get so upset, dear," looking a little bent from all the sheer female logic that Mom's been bouncing off him for seven pages. None of those soprano recitals for Harlan Cross! You know, how after all the encores, the soprano waves her hand toward the piano, and for the first time we notice this little bald guy who's been playing his fingers down to the nubs for two hours? Not me, baby!

Meanwhile, I was pretty much licking the Rick Mallory problem by memorizing both my own lines and his, so that no matter how antically he dodged around or what bizarre cues he threw me or how many times he went up I would simply keep talking—like a testimonial speaker waiting to be heckled. I became very proficient at making one line out of two: what he was supposed to say and my reply to it:

"I know you're going to ask me about the new nurse on the third floor. Her name is Miss Whitfield."

Or:

"Are you going to tell me you spoke to Paul Markham about it? If you did, why?"

Rick, in his turn, was becoming adept at letting me

know by urgent little facial ticks and eye rollings that he hadn't the foggiest notion of what to do next and for me to go right on without him. I would soliloquize madly while he did one of his little dives under the desk after a stray piece of his lines, or strove to puzzle out words on the teleprompter.

But on this particular day (one of his last), he crossed up everybody by reading *my* line off the prompter, then sitting back and waiting for a reply. This time *I* dove under the desk to keep from breaking. Rick joined me there while the cameramen took shots of the wall clock, the view out the window, the doorway.

"What's happening!" he hissed, sweat pouring off his face like rain.

"You just said my line," I said.

"What do we do now?" he said, as if there were time to draw up a plan. I've forgotten what we actually did, but I do remember—often in my sleep—that it seemed an hour before we both surfaced and began talking again.

Let it not be inferred that my picaresque misadventures with Rick Mallory were typical. The level of performing on daytime serials is very high indeed. Some of the actors have been on the show together for ten years or more, and the acting rapport they have established with each other is dazzling. These veterans can play scenes that are about stuff like roasts in the oven and Christmas trees and cheese dips and what Harry said to Thelma at Tim's birthday party with as much intensity as if they were re-enacting axe murders and suicides. If called upon to do so, they could probably hold an audience with a staged reading of the Yellow Pages.

Frances Foy, for example, who plays Ruth Markham on the show, is certainly one of the great champs of the medium. She created the role of Ruth fifteen years ago, and is a daytime TV legend in her own time. Acting classes should stop whatever they're doing every afternoon and watch Frances Foy mix a cake batter while talking her husband, Phil, into going to the doctor for a checkup. Or observe exactly how she goes about dusting and cleaning a room while advising her son, Paul, about some minutia or other of married life. That's acting, buddy!

Frances's dressing room befits legend. She has decorated it in stem-to-stern blue wallpaper, and has installed her own furniture, telephone, and coffeemaker. There are also various food tins, cooky jars, and herb teas for guests. I would expect her to be able to rustle up a cucumber sandwich, if pressed, or to produce a carafe of well-chilled wine to celebrate a sudden birth. On or off the air, she is the mother of the show: arbiter of intra-company standstills, apothecary for minor physical ills, adviser to the temporarily distraught, and general spokeswoman for the physical and moral climate of the studio.

"Hal, dear," she'll say, coming up to our producer, putting her hand on his and looking up at him with softly implacable eyes. "Steven and I were just saying how unbearably hot the studio has been getting lately. We must have air, darling, or we'll die! Yours truly and Steven—as young and strong as he is—will die, and there won't be any show. You *do* understand."

I will be forever in Frances Foy's debt for her part in helping me through the next crisis that reared its dragon's head. With Rick Mallory gone and my asthmatic knee temporarily quiescent, I had begun to envision great open vistas free of booby traps, horizons on which no storms gathered, and nights with actual sleep in them. I had not reckoned well, however.

It had been decided to bring a bad girl onto the show, eventually to be my Waterloo. Lisa. A real knockout with huge, bright eyes and flashing smile, who was on the lam from some coal-mining town where bad girls come from. Presumably having run her course playing Lola Montez among the anthracite breathers and their jealous mates, she was coming to Middletown to look up a friend who worked at Pinewood Hospital, and to start a new, if not more exemplary, life. Thus are destinies arranged. Harlan and Lisa: the bad and the beautiful.

The promise of an exotic new female coming into our midst produced no little ground-pawing among male cast members and crew. We had seen a future cast breakdown in which Lisa was described as "A knockout. Dark, sexy, very pretty, with a sensual body."

On the morning of her arrival, Gustav had worked himself up to an advanced stage of satyriasis.

"Well—today we get the sensual body!" he said, clapping his hands and hopping around like something out of an allegorical mural.

"Hoy boy!" said Tom Curtis, so caught up in the moment that he was actually standing. It was an atmosphere tense with anticipation and charged with erotic fantasy.

Our ladies, of course, were understandably reserved. Stephanie, in haircurlers and funeral snood, snorted and sniffed at the coffee machine.

"Honestly, you guys are disgusting!" she said.

Gustav tried cajoling her with a quick buss on the cheek. "Stephanie, sweetheart, we love you dearly—you are our first love. Believe me, darling, sweetie pie," he babbled goatishly, keeping one eye on the front door.

Somewhere out there a taxi was headed for our studio bearing a sleek, ripe, full-lipped goddess come to choose from among the assembled warriors. Our new knockout girl!

What finally appeared in a wet raincoat, misted eyeglasses, tossed-salad hair and galoshes was Shirley Morgan, a young actress reduced for the moment to resemble a bewildered fawn that had been separated from its mother in a forest fire.

This was Lisa? This pale, sweet, waterlogged waif with rain on her chin? We were gallant in any case. Gustav took her coat, I got coffee, and Tom, simulating enthusiasm, offered his version of a compliment.

"I'll bet you're a good kisser!"

Shirley looked up at him wanly. Remembering my own first day, I could read the sheer hysteria playing piano trills through every nerve of her body. I also noted with some alarm that the lenses of her glasses were thick enough to be bulletproof, and that when she took them off to blow her nose her large, navy blue eyes went helplessly blank like huge, windblown saucers. Stephanie whisked her off to the ladies' room for repairs, leaving the assembled warriors to ponder.

Lisa and Harlan (Shirley and I) had two long scenes together that first day: the first an introduction in the hospital cafeteria, and the second at her apartment after returning from a date that same evening.

Wearing her glasses until the run-through, Shirley managed the first part of the day with no more than the usual confusions and nervous halts, but when she took the glasses off for the run-through, hell began breaking loose. My own myopia seemed to respond to her much worse case like a sympathetic pregnancy. And presently we were staggering around together like dust-blinded legionnaires in some desert epic: spilling coffee, knocking over a chair, tripping on the stairway to her apartment, and generally behaving like a fear-crazed couple whose house is being burgled during a blackout. Sometimes another actor's nervousness can make you calmer. This wasn't one of those times. Instead I found myself re-living all the first-day horrors with her. Including the introduction to the teleprompter.

"What's in that box?" she blurted fearfully, as the teleprompter man tried to come to her rescue during a momentary dry.

"Woids!" he hissed urgently, jabbing his finger toward the machine. He might as well have offered a basketful of snakes. I could tell by her dazed expression that her "woids" had irretrievably flown from her like maddened barn swallows. Concentration shattered, we spent the rest of the scene shuffling around uncertainly like a couple of tipsy ancients playing blind man's bluff at a heart clinic's Christmas party.

Between run-through and dress rehearsal, Shirley was weeping and inconsolable.

"I'm terrified!" she cried. "I can't see anything or anything. And what was that awful box! What are 'woids'?"

I tried calming her by telling her of my own difficult first day. Gustav offered her an apple. Even Tom Curtis tried to reassure, in his fashion.

"You think it's so different for us?" he said. "Listen, the

muscles in my back are so tight right now, I can't even lift my arms!"

But it was Frances Foy who saved the situation. She took Shirley by the arm and began walking her to her dressing room.

"I understand, my dear," she said, "that you just closed in a play. You must tell me what's happening on Broadway. My God, I haven't seen a Broadway play since *The Pink Lady*." They disappeared into Frances's dressing room.

Whatever it was that Frances said to her in that enchanted cubicle, Shirley was a new girl by dress rehearsal. In costume, her hair coiffed, her curious brogans replaced by smart high-heeled pumps, and her eyes shining hotly under new lashes—Shirley became Lisa in that final hour. Gone were the baggy sweater and loose-fitting jeans. In their place, a form-fitting sheath made every move of her body a sudden and exciting promise. Where had she been hiding that lovely, full bosom! Those enchanting legs! Some divine implosion of sensuality had been set off in her. Her voice became a lustful purr:

"Harlan. I *love* that name! Har-lan." When she said the line now, her mouth became a pouting invitation.

"Jesus!" whispered Jimmy, our cameraman. "That's really something!"

Fervid suspirations of breath could be heard all over the studio. Grips and technical crew stood transfixed like religious wanderers stopping before a wayside shrine.

"What happened to the kid with the glasses?" asked Ned, our scenery painter.

"That's *her!*" said Court, our stage manager, beaming like a bemused koala bear. "Some acting, huh?"

"Some body!" said Ned.

Our knockout girl had arrived after all!

"What did you say to her in there?" I asked Frances afterwards.

"I gave her a scone and some rose hip tea and told her not to worry about a thing," answered Frances.

"What's a scone?" asked Tom Curtis, as he and Gustav joined me excitedly in my dressing room. The advent of

Lisa had established another beachhead for my story line. And what a beachhead!

"Fantastic! Gorgeous!" sputtered Gustav.

"Things didn't look so hot there until Frances came through with the tea and crumpets," said Tom. "Another break for the ass man! What a girl!"

"This bastard is really cleaning up in the story line business," added Gustav as Bill Sievers came by. Bill plays Phil Markham. Like Frances, he has been on the show since the beginning. On the show, he is just plain Phil: simple, direct, solid—with the kind of looks you expect to see on a friendly neighborhood druggist in Erie, Pennsylvania. In real life, however, Bill is a mystic with the mind and soul of an abstracted guru. I have often wondered what Phil's fans, who know him only for his country freshness, would think if they heard him describing a seance with Madame Blavatsky, or saw him riffling through tarot cards or delving into the *I Ching* with the faraway look of an enchanted Buddhist.

"Ah, yes—the story line business," said Bill. "Are you gentlemen familiar with the Hindu mandala?"

We grunted various degrees of recognition.

"I am reminded," he went on, "of the mandala when considering the phenomenon of the story line business. The logic of the circle, the final and inexorable balance and harmony." He paused as if to be sure of our attention.

"I'm listening," said Tom. "It's just that I can't look at you because of my neck."

"Your neck is bothering you? I'm sorry," said Bill.

"It's all right, I can hear you. Go on."

"Well, now, there are about fifteen leading characters on a serial, correct?"

"Yes," we said.

"And," Bill went on, "about five or so story lines dealt with over a period of a month, directly involving, let's say, eight of the fifteen characters. Which means that during a given month, seven of the characters will not have a story line, but may simply be on the scene, or involved tangentially."

Gustav, shirtless, stared at Bill like a baleful totem.

"Where is the mandala, Bill?" he said. "We are waiting patiently for the mandala."

"New characters," Bill continued, "also come in and out for weeks or months who figure in the story line as well."

"So?"

"The logistics, the shifts of emphasis, the overlapping involvements of the characters, I find very fascinating. The story goes on and on—the continuum; the final balance, harmony, the logic—reminds me of the mandala. The circular representation of deities, with the self at the center—hopefully."

"I think Tom's neck is better now," said Gustav. "Look, he's moving."

Shirley Morgan soon firmly established herself as a swinging and formidable Lisa, and what with leaping around from wee-hour gambols with her, to early morning surgery, to home busting at the Markhams', as the indefatigable Harlan Cross I began to find myself just this side of breath shortness. All those trichotomies to perform! All those cloying females! The plotting and scheming! All those lines to memorize! In one three-week period I played a total of forty-three scenes. My face had begun to take on the pallor of lemon sherbet, I was losing weight, and circles the color of faded licorice were forming under my eyes. I began coming home from the studio at night feeling as if I'd spent the day running up and down the fifteen flights to our apartment, and looking, roughly, like an emaciated albino panda.

Even my wife, Angela, who has gotten used to the special oddness of an actor's life, was taken aback.

"You don't look too good," said Angela toward my supine form as I lay gasping on the lower level of my son's double decker bed, sipping Scotch through a straw.

"That's funny," I gasped. "I slept five hours last night."

"Your eyes!" she said.

"Are they still there?"

"You look like an infected rabbit."

This confused me, because just that very morning they had looked like two dabs of leftover raspberry jello on a hospital dessert tray. Could they have changed that much?

"How many pages do you have to learn tonight?" she continued solicitously.

"Twenty-five," I answered dully. "How's Chris? Is he growing?"

"You got a pack of mail this morning."

"Mail?"

"People writing to you."

"Me? People?"

"Yes."

Fan mail is accumulated at the agency and delivered in eventual packets. My first packet! Ah! Letters from all those lovely mothers and daughters out there! Here would be words of love to knit up the raveled sleeve of care. Cool hands for my fevered brow. I tore open my packet exultantly and began to read.

What was this!

"What is this!" I cried. Hostility! Grief! Cries in the night from places I'd never heard of like Houma, Louisiana and Xenia, Ohio—imploring me to stop ruining Paul and Nancy's life. A tear-stained missive from Maple Shades, New Jersey typed on three-ring notebook paper telling me how to find God! Imprecations from Richmond, Indiana! An outright threat from Frankfort, Kentucky!

"What is this!" I cried again. "Fans? They hate me!"

"But you're just acting a part," said Angela.

"Not to them. I'm not me anymore. I'm him!" I held an ice cube to my forehead.

"I need a fresh straw!" I croaked, sending a flutter of hate letters sliding off my chest.

Thinking all the time that women out there were loving me as that marvelous baaad man when actually I had become an object of scorn and loathing! I pictured myself in local post offices:

CAUTION: HE IS HATEFUL AND PROBABLY ARMED

"But what about the broccoli girl!" I whimpered incoherently.

"The what, dear?" Angela asked kindly in a voice that

a nurse might use to an outpatient who has just told her he was a robin.

"This girl in Gristede's. Such a pretty little thing. There she was, reaching for the broccoli . . . . "

Angela unbuttoned my shirt and laid a cool hand on my brow.

"You'd better rest, dear. Then I'll wake you, and you'll have a nice steak, rare just like you like it, and a big glass of milk."

"Dinn—nner?" I stuttered, staring through drowsy rabbit eyes.

"And then you can study."

"But this girl," I persisted, "I'm not kidding. She loved me on the show. And her mother too!" More letters fluttered to the floor.

As I lay there, stunned, trying to assimilate what had happened, the phone rang. It was my mother calling long distance in some agitation.

"Hello, Mother. Yes, I can hear you fine. What? You don't want to bother me, you say? No. No. What?" My mother thinks of a long distance call as a thing to be shouted over some great gulf.

"Mrs. Jessup called me yesterday," she said. "Remember the Jessups?"

"Jessups?"

"Tommy Jessup? You were in the seventh grade together."

My brain whirled backwards, fainted several times, and then touched dimly on a fat-cheeked boy with a face like a fried egg. No. No. That was Hobie somebody—fat Hobie. Was it the skinny one? The kid with the caved-in chest and green teeth? Ruthlessly my mother waited for me to recollect the twelfth year of my life.

"That was a pretty long time ago, Mother," I murmured beatenly.

"Well, anyway," she continued, "Mrs. Jessup said how you were such a *nice* boy. And now she just can't believe you're the same person!"

"Yeah, but . . . . "

"She said the way you're trying to get Nancy to leave

Paul and have him thrown out of the hospital so you can be assistant to chief of surgery is just terrible!"

"I'm not. That's the character. Tell Mrs. Jessup I'm not doing any of that. Tell her I'm just trying to get a little shuteye here before they come for me with the cuffs and the butterfly net."

"Oh, I know," said my mother knowingly. "But what's going to happen with Lisa?"

"What?"

"Are you going to get her pregnant? Mrs. Jessup thinks you're going to get her pregnant and then she'll try to make you marry her and you'll probably desert her and get in trouble with the hospital. I told her you wouldn't do that."

"Did you?"

"But are you? That Lisa is a bad girl, Steven. She might even try to kill you or something."

"Mother, for Christ's sake!"

My own mother!

What was happening? Things were crumbling, that's what. There were cracks in the wall. Those dreams of glory—fading like old snapshots! Euphoria was out. Menace was in.

Even Gristede's became a disaster area. A few days after the phone call from my mother, a woman touched my arm as I was reaching for an avocado. I looked up and into eyes burning like coals.

"You are breaking up a wonderful home," she said, swinging at me with her pocketbook and falling forward onto her knees. One of my avocadoes fell on a toy poodle who emitted a strangled cry. Instant panic: screaming, yelping, guys with green jackets running around as I retreated out of the store. That was Tuesday.

On Wednesday, I had just spent a particularly grueling day on camera, followed by a long special rehearsal of a complicated operation to be performed the next day. Real nurses were there, as usual, to explain to us what we were doing step by tedious step. Alan Ames, who plays Paul, is a medical nut. He kept asking these interested questions and reveling in long interesting answers.

"One more question, Alan," I said under bated breath, "and these girls are going to have to explain how to get my knuckles out of your throat!"

Gustav entertained during lulls by juggling the instruments and suggesting various uses for them that got our Nightingales yelping and whooping like excited parakeets. By the time things had simmered down, and we had been sufficiently catechized about mitral valve incisions, it had become an eleven-hour day and I crawled into bed with a script to memorize and aching for sleep.

Angela was waiting for me, however, with the special set look she assumes when troubled. The look might be described as somewhere between the haughty, distracted stare of a llama and the ferocious lowering of a distempered yak.

"Those love scenes between you and Lisa are pretty convincing," she blurted.

"What?"

"What's she like?"

"What do you mean, 'what's she like?' She's a girl, a nice person," I said, trying to roll over.

"I'll bet," said Angela grimly. "And what about Nancy and that new nurse? The one with the nice legs—is she a nice person too? Yesterday she almost let that patient in intensive care die because she was messing around with you in the lab office!"

Sweet Jesus! My own wife!

"Nice person! Nice person!" Angela litanized, her voice trembling with the particular timbre it assumes when she is about to open old wounds. "That's what you said about that blonde in Los Angeles. Nice person! What are they— your code words for ravishing?"

"For God's sake," I said, my mind spinning backwards three years and three thousand miles, "that girl was a member of the company—we were doing a picture together—we became friends—it was nothing!"

"Such a good friend she called here at midnight!"

"It wasn't midnight, it was 9:00."

"In Los Angeles it was midnight!"

"Haven't you read my fan mail?" I croaked. "Women

58

hate me in Los Angeles. That one from Pasadena was practically a death threat!"

Angela turned over and was asleep in a trice. I, on the other hand, waited stoically in the dark as my mind skipped a demented tango of confused reveries: blondes in Los Angeles, stoop ball matches with fat Hobie and Tommy Jessup, death threats from Pasadena, avocadoes and yelping poodles. Including intermission the show lasted about three hours.

Groping my way to the bathroom at 6:30, my head full of steel wool shavings and my eyelids feeling as if they'd been taped to my cheekbones, I stared into the mirror. Was that the happy-go-lucky lover staring at me there? That bleary, bogus Bogart with—(what is that, a twitch?) —a twitch in my left rabbit eye? Women love *you?* Who could love a rotten homebreaker with a twitch!

Having located my chin I began to shave, trying to put out of my mind those letters—to say nothing of my chipper and humorous answers to them. But it was no use. A tape recording of them semed to be coming at me from out of the medicine chest:

> Dear Mr. Prince,
>
> I and my mother are both shocked to death by your really terrible conduct toward Paul Markham and Nancy who are our favorites on the show.
>
> Mrs. Henrietta Grotowski

(How do you stop a twitch?)

> Dear Mr. Prince,
>
> My late husband evinced tendencies such as yours in the early days of our marriage. Had it not been for our minister, heaven only knows what might have transpired . . . .
>
> Mrs. Phyllis Crosley

(An infected rabbit! Act V. Learn it in the cab. Maybe in the makeup chair. . . .)

Dear Mr. Prince:

I have been a faithful follower of the story for many years now, and never have I seen such criminal behavior as yours is . . . .

Mrs. Louise Harper

(I'm sorry! I'm sorry!)

Shaved and dressed and clutching my script, I reached the front door just as my son, Chris, appeared out of his room in pajamas and bright eyes ready to start *his* day. He was wearing his baseball mitt.

"Hey, Dad! Mr. Gorman is taking the whole class to the ball game this afternoon. The Giants are in town. Too bad you can't come!"

The image bathed over me like sunlight and warm Pacific waves: hot dogs and score cards, Willy Mays— heedless, fun-filled hours.

"I wish I could, pal," I answered cheerily. "Have fun."

Chris slapped his fist into the palm of his Whitey Ford special. "Thanks," he said, disappearing into the bathroom. I rang for the elevator wondering how they ever dropped a ball with those big, new gloves.

As the weeks went by, and Middletown continued to reel and catch its breath from my continuing assaults on its integrity, I had come to accept as fact the growing indignation of the outside world. It was everywhere: the threatening letters, the hostile glances in Bloomingdale's, the calls from my mother describing Mrs. Jessup's outrage. Even my friend Mike, at Foley's bar, whose mother had taken to hating me so much she'd thrown her hip out again. Dropping into Foley's one afternoon, after a long day on the set, I was accosted by Mike before I could get halfway through the door.

"Mother of God!" said Mike in awestruck tones. "I've never seen the old lady that mad as when you blamed that heart patient's death on Paul Markham."

"Well, I want his job at the hospital," I countered, choosing a seat at the bar. By this time I never insisted I was Steven Prince anymore. It was a lot easier being Harlan Cross.

"Yeah, but my God, man—there's ways and ways!"

"When you want something badly enough, Mike, you go after it."

Mike raced around the bar feverishly, like a distraught witness itching to tell his version of the accident.

"But you know yourself the boy had nothing to do with that man's death. My mother told me it was you pretending you hadn't said you'd cover for him that night when he had to go home on account of Nancy being so upset."

"Well," I hemmed equivocally.

"Now that's the God's truth. When you heard that man died you slipped out of the hospital so's you could later say you weren't on that night, and that it was Paul's responsibility. My mother told me that now, and she's no liar!"

"Listen," I said, "that son of a bitch, Markham, has had it soft all his life! He didn't have to drive a cab at night to pay his way through med school. He's had everything handed to him. So now let's see if he can stand a little heat!"

"Yeah, but . . . . " began Mike, his eyes widening.

"I didn't ask Nancy Markham to fall for me," I went on heatedly, "she just did. She's bored with that goody goody gumdrop she's married to! She wants me because she wants a real man!"

"Mother of God!" muttered Mike.

I advanced on the balls of my feet, matador fashion, poising a beer glass in my hand.

"I'm going to the top, see! And I haven't got time to wonder if I've followed all the rules. Or worry about what bartenders and their mothers think!"

Mike's face, normally a simple map of Ireland, became an aerial view of a peat bog.

"Too busy," I repeated, my voice going higher, "too busy to worry about goody gumdrops! And if a few people get hurt, a few Paul Markhams bite the dust, a few barflies fall off their stools and get funny hips—that's too bad!"

"Mary and Joseph!" said Mike, his forearms hanging at his sides like French bread loaves.

"So just keep sending those letters," I said. "Go on, keep it up!"

"What letters is that?" said Mike.

"You think a few letters can stop Harlan Cross? Don't cross Harlan Cross." I lunged at him, the glass falling loudly, and over we went into the sawdust. Foley, the owner, came running down from his office.

"What the sweet hell is this!" he said, grabbing at us.

I got to my feet in a confetti of wood shavings, waving my arms and declaiming. "Some are born great, some achieve greatness, and some have greatness thrust upon them!" I said, moving to the door.

Mike stood gaping, sawdust hanging off him, looking like a felled ox in a snowstorm.

"Shakespeare," said Mike.

"Completely," said Foley, who doesn't hear too well.

Dreamily and wearily, I headed home in a taxi. What a funny thing to happen, I remember thinking as I replayed the escapade in my mind's eye.

At dinner that night, my hands shook. Peas kept rolling off my fork. My goddam knee started to squeak. (What was all that at Foley's? What was happening?)

"How did the day go?" asked Angela. Chris was watching my fork and pea act. Even the cat was looking at me.

"Tough operation today," I said abstractedly, attacking my lamb chops with one hand and holding my knee down with the other. "Very tough. Getting at those mitral and pulmonary valves, you know."

"Mitral valves?" asked Chris.

"In the heart, see—these valves," I said.

"Is that your knee, Steven?" Angela asked, shifting.

"Yeah, sorry."

"Is that Charley?" said Chris, looking under the table for our terrier.

"No," I said. "That's my knee. And leave it alone! Big argument with Paul Markham in the scrub room today too," I continued.

"Oh?"

"He knows I'm trying to do him in with Nevins now,

and he's going to start to fight back. Tomorrow he goes to Nevins and accuses me of being a liar."

"What are you going to do, Dad?" asked Chris.

"Oh, I'll get out of it," I said, grabbing my knee as it started for the kitchen. "I can take care of Markham!" I said, yanking at my cuff under the table. "But Lisa is really giving me a hard time now. Aggressive. Very aggressive."

"Do they give vacations on these shows?" asked Angela suddenly.

The phone rang. My knee jumped off the chair and raced for the hallway. I followed it and picked up the receiver. It was my mother.

"I hate to bother you, Steven," she said, "but today— *today*, Steven!"

"I know, I was pretty bad today."

"Honestly, Steven, they are going to lock you up if you don't stop!"

"What did Mrs. Jessup think of the way I lied to Nevins about that progress report on Mr. Cushing?"

"She was *so* upset!"

"I'll bet she was," I concurred.

"And," said my mother, lowering her voice to a hushed outrage, "what must poor Angela think of those love scenes with Nancy and Lisa?"

"She's been pretty terrific about it, actually," I said.

"What's going to happen when Paul finds out what you've told Dr. Nevins about him?"

"He's going to fight back this time," I said.

"Please be careful, Steven!"

"I will, Mother. And thanks."

(Quasimodo!)

FOUR

Just as I was settling for the fictive life of unrelieved depravity, getting all those evil closing-shot smiles just right and learning how to field the disapprobation of the twelve million faithful, fate stepped in. New writers!

When you consider that the writers have to turn out a half-hour show five days a week—the physical equivalent of writing fifty-two full-length plays a year—it's no wonder new ones have to be got now and again. Like new sparkplugs.

But somehow I'd never really thought too much about it. Nobody ever sees the writers. One imagines them living in isolated, pain-wracked eyries in places like Syracuse or Chicago—chained to typewriters amid reams of paper and communicating with each other in pre-symbolic grunts. It is assumed that they rarely see the light of day, and that their eyes, narrowed to pinpoints, shine unnaturally like expiring tapers. Having no time to eat, they doubtlessly subsist on cigarettes, coffee, and intravenous dosages of carrot juice. With no occasion to dress, they spend their lives in robes and slippers, shuffling unshaven from to bed to writing table and back to bed again—knowing only by the frosty nose of their postman that winter has come, or by the distant cheeping of a finch that it is spring. Very occasionally, and weather permitting, they can be glimpsed standing under a full moon—seeming to be recalling their youth—silent and unmoving, like commemorative statuary.

What, I wondered, was happening to the old writers? What had they done? And what about the fresh, new ones? And what did all this mean about the story line?

But such secrets, I was told, lie sacred and undivulged in the breasts of a very few. It is rumored that future story lines are kept in vaults at the bottom of deserted mine shafts somewhere in West Virginia; and that conferences affecting plans for the program are held aboard ship in neutral waters off the Bahamas.

Much later I was to learn what had been decided out there in the Bahamas. My character was to be reclaimed and set right, through some offstage agony. There would be a death in the family and I would take a one-week leave from Pinewood to attend to troubled kin—thus effecting a spiritual face-lift comparable to Attila the Hun being converted at a revivalist meeting.

Rather than having all this revealed to me outright, the truth of it crept upon me like the fog on little cat's feet. As I continued on my rapacious way among virgin nurses and hammering away at Paul Markham's reputation and his bride's crumbling resolve, whispers came to me, intimations, provocative innuendoes—change was in the wind.

Here, for example, is a scene of classic foreshadowing. Lisa, my corrupt inamorata, is announcing to me that she is leaving town—and why:

Lisa
It's no good, Harlan. I've run my course in Middletown. Just like I ran it in Bayville.

Harlan
What do you mean?

Lisa
You think we're alike, don't you? Two wrong-side-of-the-trackers having to cheat and lie our way across those tracks. Well, I still am. But you're on the right side of

those tracks now. You're a brilliant surgeon, Harlan, and if you know what's good for you, you'll wake up and see you don't have to beat and claw anymore. You're there. I'm not very smart, but I'm smart enough to know that. I still have to play the old games, but you don't. So you see, we're not the same really. I mean . . . . (*Having trouble finding the words*)

                              Harlan
What? What, Lisa?

                               Lisa
I mean, you have a choice.

                              Harlan
A choice? (*He considers what Lisa has said. Then tries to dismiss it from his mind*) You don't really believe that stuff, do you? Look, I don't want you to leave. I like you. I need you.

                               Lisa
(*Resisting him*) I like you too, Harlan. You know how much. That's the main reason I'm leaving.

                              Harlan
That's crazy!

                               Lisa
No, it isn't. It's right. Right for both of us, but for different reasons . . . .

Something was up all right. Here was Lisa, a girl with an avocado pit for a heart, suddenly coming on like Doris Day. What was all that sudden helpful wisdom? Leaving? Where were they taking her? My knockout girl! And what about all that new reflectiveness in Harlan? What was all that?

Then, suddenly, there was the telegram from Europe. (Europe?) A death in the Harlan Cross family. (I had a family?) They didn't say exactly who died. Just some unmentionable death in the family. Dr. Nevins would give me a week off.

A week off! Curiously, the connection was late in dawning. I, Steven Prince, frayed of nerve and exhausted of body, could go someplace too! Ho, boy! Ahead of me yawned nine blissful days of rest! Peace! Quiet!

With the look of someone teetering down the gangplank of a returning troop ship I appeared at my front door, a wan, incredulous smile carved on my face, and tottered toward Angela.

"Think of it!" I muttered, sinking into her embrace. "Nine days!"

"You mean, off?" she said.

"Yes," I exulted collapsedly. "Harlan has to go to Europe. Death in the family."

"When?"

"Next week. Let's go to Nahawk!"

Nahawk is a blessedly obscure, Victorian-looking resort run by a marvelous Quaker family. It is named after some long-extinct Indian tribe, and is situated in upstate New York. Two thousand acres of trails and paths, a beautiful lake, Sky Mountain, and (best of all) silence—an idyllic quietude broken only by birds and crickets. It is a place we repair to now and again to have ravaged nerves restrung and heads emptied of the fumes and jungle noises of the city.

I spent the week in giddy anticipation. Nine days with no lines to memorize, no studio traumas, no 6 a.m. alarm clock janglings, no telephones to answer. Agent and lawyer would intercept the outside world and keep it at bay. Peace! Tranquillity!

"Ah!" I sighed audibly as I stared through the train window at the Hudson River shimmering hugely in the sun. Waiting for us were walks around the lake before breakfast, lolling in tiny thatch-roofed huts overlooking green vistas of valleys and mountain peaks, reading dog-eared volumes of Byron and Shelley in the early morning sun, and long, lazy afternoon hikes on mossy, pine-needled paths—trees of all sorts—mountain laurel and rhododendron and wildflowers.

"Ah!" I repeated, as I began dozing off to the rhythmic clacking of the train wheels, my weary body sinking luxuriously into the soft, plush Pullman chair. I love trains.

Limousine and driver met us at the station to take us up the mountain to the hotel.

"You folks up for the conference?" asked our driver with a welcoming smile.

"Conference?" I said dimly. We drove in silence.

"Conference?" Angela whispered, turning toward me, her eyes wide with premonition.

A week-long conference of the Women's National Auxiliary Horticulture Society was in full swing at the hotel. Our dear Nahawk was suddenly crawling with a hundred jolly female conventioneers in flowered prints and white brogans.

I had barely signed our names to the register when a shriek went up from a small gaggle of fun seekers emerging together from the gift shop. "Dr. Cross!" they fairly screamed and charged, one of them brandishing a golf putter as if, cheerily, to beat me to death.

From that moment, word of the exotic presence of the baaad doctor among the more common flora and fauna made peace and quiet a forgotten dream. I was to be inundated by floods of excited warmth. Top-heavy ladies in kimonos pursued me down corridors of the hotel. Large groups would surround our table at mealtime. Deputized cabals snuck out from behind trees or cornered me in the library for spontaneous symposiums on Harlan Cross's terrible conduct toward Paul and Nancy as contrasted to the obviously benign and blinking presence of Steven Prince, who somehow (oh, magically!) *was* that mad, bad doctor on the TV screen.

At night, as I strove to sleep in the unaccustomed quiet, notes rustled under the door. Excited tappings jarred me awake at odd hours.

On the third afternoon, having escaped from two strapping dowagers in space shoes who challenged me to a walking race, I set myself up in a flat-bottomed canoe in the middle of the lake—lazily drifting and casting for rainbow trout. The soft whine and purr of the line as I cast out and reeled in, and the gentle water lapping against the side of the boat were the only sounds to be heard out there. Adrift in the peaceful sunlight, my work-torn soul sighed thankfully. Ah, peace!

Lazing back and allowing my line to troll, I half-closed my eyes and listened to the trees.

Suddenly, a head bobbed up out of nowhere—a face with cordovan skin and close-cropped steel-gray hair like wet Brillo flashed up out of the water.

"AHHH!" I yelped.

"Ahoy there, doctor!" came an olive-gray female voice.

I dropped my fishing pole in the water. Down she went after it, gurgling undinely. Then up she came again, the pole held triumphantly in one hand, and began spraying questions at me about Middletown, Pinewood Hospital, the Hippocratic oath.

I gamely rowed away from her toward the dock, but she swam right along with me, telling me between watery gasps that her father had been (besides being a hell of a guy) a top surgeon in Philadelphia—a really good, true-to-the-Hippocratic-oath guy. Not like Harlan Cross, whose (did I mind if she spoke frankly?) conduct in and out of Pinewood Hospital was—well, frankly frightful. She said that fishing had always bored her and that archery was *her* sport, and that she had done quite a bit of acting with the Thespis Society in Philadelphia and would love to do some acting on TV. Was it hard to get on TV? She imagined it was. Had I ever heard of the Thespis Society in Philadelphia? No, I confessed, turning the boat around with a farewell shout and rowing like hell in the opposite direction, I had never heard of the Thespis Society in Philadelphia.

With three powerful backstrokes she was abreast of me in a trice. Last season she had played Banquo in an all-female production of *Macbeth,* and had directed her own adaptation of an Iris Murdoch novella. With each powerful stroke some new bit of narrative would suggest itself to her.

My arms began to feel as if they were coming out of their sockets and I was wheezing and puffing like an asthmatic water buffalo. Sensing my distress, she volunteered to pull me into shore which, despite my feeble protests, she proceeded to do—holding the boat rope in her left hand and executing a powerful side stroke with her right.

A group of her flower lady pals, on the porch which looks out over the dock, cheered and applauded as we pulled into port.

"We made it, chaps!" said my Banquo lady up at them, then leaped onto the deck, fastened the rope, and lifted me—paralyzed and limp armed from rowing—out of the boat. The horticulture ladies cheered again as I slipped and fell on the wet mooring.

"You can do better than that, doctor!" yelled one of them with the voice of a giant tern attacking a school of herring. I scrambled to my feet with a feeble wave of my hand and ran brokenly toward my room—wild rhythmic applause receding behind me—a diminishing thunder of— what? Love? Hate?

As I lay face down on the bed, my arms dangling to the floor like chunks of pulled taffy, Chris, who had watched the whole spectacle from the porch, regaled Angela with my adventure.

"Gee, Mom, you should have seen this skinny old lady lift Dad right out of the boat!"

"I couldn't move," I mumbled into my pillow; "my arms were frozen."

"Nice going, tiger," purred Angela.

At supper, a delegation headed by the Banquo lady presented themselves at our table.

"We've never actually been introduced—I'm Amanda Chisholm," she said, pumping my hand powerfully. Lean and ageless, she stood about 6′ 1″ in her no-nonsense Thom McAn pumps. Behind her a small, round woman with pince-nez glasses, who looked as if she might have been invented by Ben Franklin, inched forward.

"That was quite a performance out on the dock this afternoon, doctor!" she said impishly. I could tell from her voice it was the giant tern lady. "Goodness, you're not at all like you are on the TV!"

The group began inching toward me with different little friendly commands.

"Take off your glasses, doctor!"

"Stand up."

"Pretend you're operating," said a voice, handing me my knife and fork and brandishing a camera. Backed against the wall, my hands cupped instinctively over my lower abdomen, I made small waves with my nose toward the table where my dinner was getting cold.

"You haven't eaten!" roared a solicitous voice from the back row.

"The doctor hasn't eaten!"

"Let the doctor eat!"

I made crazy little head nods.

"We won't keep you," said Amanda Chisholm. "I'll get right down to business. Your fans—that's us," she clarified with a wave toward the group, "would be most honored if you would go caving with us tomorrow morning."

"Yes!" yelled a peppy voice in the rear.

"Caving!" There was a chorus of cheers.

"Let the doctor eat," repeated the solicitous lady.

"Wait a minute," commanded Amanda Chisholm. There was a hush. "There are some wonderful caves in this area. We'll supply the caving suit and the candles and ropes—all you have to bring is a pair of sneakers."

"And yourself!" added the tern lady puckishly.

"Yes!" said the peppy one. They pushed forward, tensely waiting for confirmation.

"Caving?" I said, fighting for time.

"Then it's settled," said Amanda Chisholm. A loud cheer.

"Well, I . . . . "

But they were gone.

I stared at their happy retreating figures and then down at my food—a cold, gelid still life against the white cloth. The kitchen was closing up. Chris gallantly offered me half a roll.

"What are you going to do?" whispered Angela, as we prepared for bed.

"I can't go on any caving trip, for Christ's sake," I whispered, glancing furtively at the open transom above our door and devouring a maple sugar man picked up in the gift shop. "I can hardly move my arms!"

"I know," said Angela, "you *should* rest. But they *are* your fans, and it means so much to them."

"That's true," I agreed. "They don't seem to hate me at all."

"They love you."

"Love me, yes. That's true," I mused. A note shot under the door. "Remember tomorrow," it said, and was signed "Amanda Chisholm."

I tossed and turned for hours, my empty stomach growling furiously, my head churning with guilty schemes of how to elude the flower ladies. One thing was sure: there was to be absolutely no caving trip. I would sneak out early, escape around the farther side of the lake, take my lake walk, come back and breakfast in my room. Yes, that was it! Then take a nap. Ho, boy! And later I would say I'd slept late—not feeling awfully well—something like that. Yes, good! Of course, they might pull a fast one of some kind. What about that? Maybe room service would wheel in the breakfast table and they'd come spilling out from under it like midgets in a circus car. How about that! I listened for wall tappings, and peered expectantly at the slit of light under the door for another note. Possibly a plan change. Sky diving over Bear Mountain maybe? Helicopter racing? The sound of crickets magnified into possible horticulture fans climbing up the latticework to our balcony.

With little sleep I arose at dawn, weary and starved, and tiptoed guiltily down the hall—down a back stairway, out into the dewy morning sunshine. With occasional glances over my shoulder I broke into a sprint, got across the wooden bridge and onto the path that rims the lake— my arms held away from my body so as not to jostle them. Slowing to a giddy jog, I kept going along the lake path, hunting for a secluded, green, mossy spot on the farther side.

Ah, there it was—hidden from the path by a large

beech tree—and at its center, a lovely, gently sloping rock, time-worn into a smooth and cozy hollow. I stretched out on it like a contented lizard, soaking in the early morning sunshine, smelling the air, and rubbing life back into my arms. Ah, perfect! Above me the blue sky, and at my feet the water softly lapping at the shore. Trees rustled in the soft breeze. A robin looked at me, opened the small brown fan of its wing, then hopped away. Bobwhites whistled overhead.

In a half-hour there would be breakfast. Thin, delicate wheat cakes dripping with melted butter and real maple syrup! Thick, juicy link sausages, honey buns, country coffee and thick cream. I chortled in the sunshine—happy and decisive. Absolutely no caving trip. No, sir. Still, I mused on smilingly, it *was* nice of them to want me to go —touching, really. Growing expansive, I began to politely include them in later-in-the-week plans: perhaps we would join them on the beach for a swim one afternoon. Yes, good. Good idea. After all, they *are* fans and they really seem to love me. Nice ladies—sweet ladies. No caving trips or anything like that; perhaps a little chat on the beach. Good. Good idea. Good thinking. Ha! Ha! Sausages! Beautiful!

A sudden sound shattered my reverie. I leaped up and spun around numbly. Silently, stealthily, like surrounding Indians, a battery of ladies in caving suits loomed out of the dew from behind mimosa bushes—moving, circling, coming closer.

"Here we are!" called Amanda Chisholm, moving in on me and waving a pair of denim overalls. Caught! An instinctive desire to run, combined with a split-second decision not to, produced a stumbling sideways shuffle— as if I were going into a sudden soft shoe routine.

"We've found you!"

I made a small honking sound, acknowledging.

"You hadn't forgotten, had you?" she went on in a dark gray voice. "Here, slip this on."

"Wait!" I said, my voice a panicky chirp. "What about breakfast?"

"Best not to eat before," she countered wisely.

"I need nourishment—eat—hungry!" I jabbered.

"We have sandwiches for later," overruled Amanda Chisholm. "And some very special things for when you're *really* hungry," she added, tapping her large basket proudly.

"I'm really hungry right now," I said.

"Discipline the body, doctor!" she announced with a ferocious slap at her lean, flat middle. Then she tapped the basket again. "It will all taste so much better later."

I made another honking noise and stepped beatenly into my caving suit.

In a trice we were hurling ourselves up a steep incline, shortcutting to a narrow uphill path.

"It's about a mile to Newland's Cave," said Amanda, grabbing me heartily and sending a ripple of pain through my rowing arm. "We'll do that one first."

"First?" I said, my stomach rumbling ominously.

"Then there's a tougher one down by Giant's Workshop. We'll need the ropes for that. We'll tackle it after lunch."

"Lunch? What?" I disbelieved. "But I've got to get back to the hotel for lunch." Was I dreaming all this?

"Not really time. Don't worry, I left a note for your wife not to expect us," she concluded vigorously. To the right appeared a sudden clearing between pine trees down mossy rocks toward the lake path. Glancing furtively, I wondered for a wild moment if I could accidentally fall down it without breaking anything.

But just then a small, squat lady with strawberry hair tied in a bun bubbled up behind us.

"Oh, doctor, it's such a pleasure having you with us!" she said, taking my other rowing arm. I turned my wince into a quick smile. "You know, you're so different in person."

(I shouldn't just run away. They really *are* nice. The strawberry lady caring about what I'm really like. That *is* nice.)

"That's nice of you," I said to the strawberry lady.

"This is Miriam," said Amanda. "Miriam is head of the Providence chapter."

"Rhode Island," said Miriam, clarifying. "I do hope

that you find some eligible woman in Middletown who might help you. Lisa is leaving, of course, and Nancy— well . . . ." She allowed her voice to trail charitably.

"Yes, thank you," I said, wondering if it would be too girlish to simply pretend to pass out at their feet and let them carry me back, sling-chair fashion, to the hotel.

After considerable scampering through increasingly rugged terrain we reached the mouth of Newland's cave.

"Isn't it wonderful to have a big baaad man with us!" said the giant tern lady coming up from the rear and staring zestfully into the wet, craggy funnel.

"Is there a doctor in the house?" jested Miriam of the Providence chapter with a high, Schrafftsy giggle.

Amanda distributed candles and we "lit up." "The doctor will bring up the rear," she said, plunging into the inky void.

The last of a series of estimable rears bumped downward into the gloom. Here was my chance to run like hell! But wait—lose all that nice love? And there was the sheer disgrace to think about. Feathers would probably be slid under our door. Threats. Letters to *The Times*. Headlines in the horticulture bulletin:

TELEVISION DOCTOR DESERTS CHAPTER HEADS
COWARDLY BEHAVIOR SCORED BY MEMBERSHIP

And there were Angela and Chris to consider. I squeezed down into the darkness.

Bumping, groaning, crawling, shoving, my rowing arms tingling with pain, I urged myself through the wet, pitch-black labyrinth. During pauses for breath-catching, the tern lady and the peppy one huffed questions at me about the show.

"Is Nancy going to stay with Paul?" asked the peppy one, her candle throwing an eerie nimbus of light on our moist faces.

"Looks that way," I said, staring vacantly through dirt-caked lenses.

"You and that naughty Lisa!" clucked the tern lady saltily, nudging my shoulder with her candle hand.

"Is she coming back?"

"Don't know," I said trying to drown out the loud roaring growls of my empty stomach and gamely to propel myself without undue use of my unhappy arms.

"Is Dr. Nevins married in real life?"

"Is Nancy going to have a baby? She seems heavier."

"What's Frances Foy really like?"

"Brave lads!" exhorted Amanda from up front somewhere.

Puffing, wet, dirt encrusted, and dripping with wax, we finally emerged—what seemed like a day later. Squinting furiously at the blast of sunlight, I threw myself down into some ferns. My arms lay pulsing on either side of me, aching and vicious.

"Fascinating example of lateral glacial erosion!" said Miriam, puffing up to me excitedly with a plastic bag of "the special things for later." "And such stratified drift!"

I nodded, grabbing at the plastic bag. On top was a small head of Bibb lettuce.

"Wha dis?" I slurred incredulously.

"Organic vegetables!" said Miriam proudly. Under the lettuce, a wad of dandelion greens, four radishes, and a tomato.

"Wha?"

"And there's a sandwich there somewhere," she said, helping.

"Wha?"

"Here we are!" she said, producing a cucumber sandwich on moist slices of wheat germ bread.

I retreated into fantasy: Angela seated prettily in some sun-drenched gazebo lustily eating juicy sausages. Then in a canoe, under a lacy parasol, being rowed and sung to by a strong, happy-armed Italian and devouring waffles dripping with melted butter.

"Ready for the Giant's Workshop?" inquired Amanda rhetorically.

Newland's Cave had been a beginner's slope. Giant's Workshop offered "Broken Head" cave, picaresquely named after some Indian who had undoubtedly become extinct trying to get out of it. A bottomless pit full of treacherous dead-end turns, spider's nests, crumbling rocks, and groin-rending apertures got through only by Herculean shovings and haulings. Our groans filled the air like Muzak.

My hair was set on fire briefly. And shortly after, as I strove to wedge her through a crevice, the peppy lady fell backwards, zonking me above the jaw with her elbow, and sending us on a long, sprawling slide. Something that sounded like a little short drum roll went on inside my collarbone, as I pillowed her fall.

"Oh, dear! Oh, I'm so sorry!"

"That's OK," I managed, noting by my freely thrashing left leg that another abyss yawned just stage left of where we had landed. We'd lost our candles somewhere.

"Is that you, doctor?" Her voice came in urgent gasps, as we struggled to untwine from a previously unknown Karma Sutra position.

With a free hand, I fondled what I imagined to be a sure fracture of the left cheekbone. A sharp pain ran up my arm, reminding me of the shoulder. It was pitch black.

"Help!" I yelled. No use kidding around. "Help!"

There was rope tying in the dark, and a lot of hauling. A brief physical examination conducted at the mouth of the cave by Amanda Chisholm determined that nothing had been broken.

"My father taught me a lot about bones, doctor."

I was a wonderful sport. The best. A veritable gallant. A hero.

"You're a hero, doctor," confided the tern lady, as we beat our way back toward the hotel. Earlier there had been a kiss of gratitude from the peppy lady.

I was deposited at the door of my room, songs of praise and affection receding dimly down the corridor as I fumbled with lock and key.

The next four days, as I try to recollect them, pass in a confused reverie of sudden-death golf playoffs, geological field trips, and swimming races. Friday afternoon the ladies announced the "Dr. Harlan Cross Mountain Climb" —named in my honor. Eight hundred feet up the sheer face of Sky Mountain with ropes and pitons.

Amanda Chisholm and a delegation of four waited outside our room. As I remember it, they had given me five minutes to make up my mind about going on the climb. And believe me, they weren't kidding around. Angela and I held an urgent whispered conference in the bathroom.

"I don't know if I can make it," I said. "I can hardly drag my body around, much less up."

"It *is* frightening," agreed Angela.

"On the other hand," I reasoned, "they've rented all that equipment."

"Made arrangements for the guide and all."

"Yes! What'll I do?"

"You *have* held up amazingly so far."

"And they named it after me."

"They *are* dear. Such devoted fans. It *is* an honor."

"They love me. They'd be so hurt."

"I could tell them you were sick."

"No, no! They'd be in here with organic vegetable soup and everything!"

"Do you think you can make it?"

"One more day."

"My dear!" Her lip was trembling.

"Of course, I could be killed."

"Oh, Steven!" She was crying. "Please be careful!"

The climb took five and a half hours. Angela and Chris, who watched the ascent breathlessly through heavy binoculars, agreed that there were only two or three times when it seemed as if I were falling freely. The other times looked more like brief slips or short slides.

That night I was intermittently delirious and apparently called out loudly several times during the two or three hours I actually slept. I was running a fever and my body ached so badly the hotel doctor had to come in and give me a shot.

"This man needs a complete rest," he said. I made a burbling sound and motioned for Angela and the doctor to come closer. They leaned down over the bed. "I'm finished," I said.

"Oh, I'm so proud of you!" said Angela in a hoarse,

urgent whisper. "But you can't quit now. What about the party?"

"Party?" I said slowly.

"The flower ladies have planned a farewell party for you tonight."

"They love me," I said.

"Yes, dear."

"Then we can go home."

"Yes, dear."

Leaning heavily on Amanda's arm, I made it to the ballroom. One hundred voices lifted to "He's a jolly good fellow." There was a gigantic cake with "To Our Favorite Doctor" written on it. Amanda presented me with an honorary membership scroll of the society. As she did, she kissed me shyly on the cheek and a loud cheer went up. I made a short speech. Another cheer. There was square dancing, in which Angela and Chris joined spiritedly. I sat and watched, smiling wanly like an aged dignitary. Certainly I would never forget my flower ladies. And in a crazy way I would miss them.

On Sunday afternoon they were there—all of them, to say goodbye. As the limousine waited to drive us to the train and Chris helped me into the back seat, the peppy lady burst forward bearing a large bon voyage box laden with fruits and flowers, on the top a large rutabaga man on which she had sewn a green operating gown of organic dandelion greens. A note said, "We love you," and was signed "The Girls." As the car started I made a final wave out the window, held myself together until we rounded the curve, then collapsed against the mercifully plush leather.

FIVE

When we got home, the doorman handed me a package of scripts. Somehow I had to be back at the studio the next morning. I felt as if I'd been scraped off the bottom of a deserted houseboat. Except for particular parts of me that ached there was a pervasive numbness, as if I'd been given a random series of local anesthetics. My face burned and swollen, and fighting to keep awake, I lay like a propped corpse leafing through the script and trying to rally myself into memorizing.

The new writers had apparently wasted no time finding me a new lady friend to match what was obviously to be my new image. Magically, as if she had been there at Pinewood Hospital right along, there was to be a devoted young internist—a Dr. Susan Williams, described on page twenty-four as:

> *Young, attractive, refined. Her manner is quiet and shy. Thoroughly devoted to her profession, hers has been a life free of personal indulgence. Despite her rather contained exterior, however, there is an unguessed-at depth of personality and feeling.*

Before long the words started dancing around the page like trained fleas. Struggling, I fell into a drugged sleep. But not for long.

Presently I was back in Newland's Cave. Air time was 3:30 and I had missed the dress rehearsal. With a candle in one hand and my half-learned script in the other, I was desperately crawling on aching arms toward the light. "Got to get out of here!" I was shouting. The peppy lady was cueing me. Distantly I could hear the hollow voice of Court, our stage manager, calling places. How was I going to operate on a patient in this rotten caving suit? I had taken a wrong turn somewhere! Court's voice grew dimmer, calling out the seconds: fifteen, then ten, then five! "Wait!" I screamed. "Wait! Wait!" and thrashed to consciousness in a cold and clammy sweat.

Scant hours later I hailed my post-dawn taxi and collapsed into the back seat. When I gave the studio address, my driver looked at me quizzically.

"That ain't the hospital. The hospital's two blocks north." My features distorted with sun and windburn, my left leg dragging noticeably, my arms hanging limply like strands of deck rope, I hobbled past the reception desk unrecognized either by Claire, the receptionist, or Tim, the caretaker. To spare them, I joggled past to the elevator.

Frances Foy was in, and I went straight to her dressing room.

"Frances, it's me," I said.

"Who? Oh, God! Oh, my dear!" she said, reaching for restorative herbs among her shelves. Camomile tea with wheat germ and honey was followed by a back rub. In a failing voice, I outlined my adventures.

Frances took my arm and guided me to the makeup room. I stood in the doorway, dumbly waiting for recognition.

"Everybody," announced Frances, commanding attention, "Steven is back." Heads lifted, eyebrows arched, looks incredulized.

"Jesus!" said Tom Curtis, leaping uncharacteristically to his feet.

"Steven?" said Stephanie, ducking out from under the hairdryer. Her face froze into an expression of dazed wonderment. "Steven?" she repeated less certainly.

"Steven, sweetheart!" said Gustav, rising out of his *Times* crossword. "Is it really you?" Carl, the makeup man, went into a frenzy. There is a certain kind of frenzy peculiar to makeup men when challenged. I was the challenge.

"My God, you look like the portrait of Dorian Gray, or something!" he yelled, running to the closet for a towel. "What do you think I am—a plastic surgeon?" Soaking the towel in steaming hot water, he continued to sputter vituperations. "Jesus! I thought you were someone coming in here to sell pencils! Or check the meter or something!" He was addressing the room now. "Call *that* a star!" he taunted rhetorically. "Is that a *face!* Looks more like two pounds of chopped chuck!" He proceeded to bandage my face with the steaming towel, expertly leaving me a hole the size of a quarter to sputter and gasp through, and a slit for my left eye.

Woodenly ensconced in a sling chair facing the door, I let one eye stare at the misty figures of my colleagues and wondered about getting through the day.

"I'll get back to you later; just sit there and be quiet," said Carl. "Come on, Steph." Stephanie got up into the makeup chair.

"Was he in a fight?" asked Tom.

"No," answered Frances. "He fell in a cave. Or was it off a mountain?"

"Off a mountain!" boomed Gustav. "Ah! There's sport for you! I was climbing once in Innsbruck with my first wife—no, my second wife. And she fell also. She broke her arm and was quite furious. It was marvelous!"

Once Carl had got the towel around my face it was business as usual in the makeup room: everyone waiting to be made up, ladies having their hair done, delivery people popping in with cans of hair spray or sandwiches from around the corner. Alan Ames, the medicine nut who plays Paul Markham, ran in in his track suit. (He's also a health nut, and likes to run around the block and eat yogurt.) He asked if he could borrow the towel off my face. Pepe, the hairdresser, was on the phone wrangling tickets out of somebody for the ball game. Hal, our producer, ran in and told a joke and ran out again. Tom Curtis started complaining about his neck. The day was starting to pick up steam. Sitting with a towel around my face wasn't enough to make it stop.

Terry, our production assistant, was at the door. "Everybody," she said, signaling an announcement, "this is Jennifer Dryden. She's playing Dr. Susan Williams." There was a cacophony of greeting.

Jennifer Dryden didn't just walk into the room, she burst upon it as if out of a huge birthday cake. In a voice that evoked the meow of a baby puma, she spoke her first words. "It's really cool to meet you all," she said. "I mean, I've seen the show and like I think you're all just groovy." Everyone made small, disclaiming cello sounds. Peering through my towel, I focused on where the kitten noises were coming from. Under the terracotta felt beret, tilted rakishly down over one eye, there was a Botticelli face and long blond hair. A floor-length leather maxi coat was hanging open, revealing a beige see-through net mini dress clinging desperately to her body. I wondered what was in the larger-than-life Gucci tote bag, and decided on a Yorkshire terrier and two midgets.

Jennifer threw her coat on the couch and surveyed the room. Standing at rigid attention, Gustav and Tom stared fixedly. There didn't seem to be much under the beige see-through net mini dress except generous expanses of Jennifer Dryden. This was Dr. Susan Williams? With the "contained personality"? Where, I wondered through my towel, was the "unguessed-at feeling behind the shy and quiet exterior"?

"I know you," she said, turning languid eyes on Gustav, "you played all those Indians and Nazi generals and things on the late show." Gustav bowed uncertainly, wondering, as Jennifer let her voice hang in midair, whether she was through with him. She was.

"Wow—it's like early, isn't it," she said, letting herself down into the couch, crossing her long, strong legs, opening her Gucci bag and withdrawing a bit of animated fluff. "Cyrano couldn't believe it when I woke him up this morning." (I'd been wrong. It was a poodle. But I was still betting on the midgets.)

"What happens now?" she purred, throwing her legs over an arm of the couch and nestling Cyrano in her see-through lap.

"They'll call you," said Frances politely, moving with dignity to the door. With appropriate "excuse me" sounds, Gustav and Tom stole out after her.

"See you later!" Jennifer said with a careless toss of her vividly Sassooned head.

"You don't remember me, right?" she said, settling deeper into the couch. I looked around to see who was left in the room.

"I mean *you*," she said with a beginning smile.

"Me?" I said through my towel. "Remember you?"

"Yayus," she said, flexing and turning Southern.

"I don't remember very much today," I said.

"I'd know you anywhere, towel or no towel," she said.

"You would? How?"

"Hands," she said.

"Hands?"

"You have like very beautiful hands."

"Is that so?" I said, trying not to look down at them.

"I dig extremities," she said.

"You do?"

"I've seen you operate."

"Really?"

"On TV."

"Oh."

"The first time I saw your hands, I like *knew* right away. I mean remembered. Even with your mask on and every-thing. Of course, I've seen you on Broadway too. But you don't remember *me*, do you?"

"I'm afraid I don't. Your hands or anything," I said.

"Well, I looked different then."

"That must be it," I said, struggling foggily behind my towel.

"Long, mousey hair and braces on my teeth and like a little pudgy."

"I can't imagine you pudgy," I said.

"Well—*plump*. I guess you'd say I was plump," she said, shifting her hips slightly.

"Where was this?" I asked.

"Westport. I was an apprentice and you came in to do a tryout of a new play called *One for the Road*."

"Well I'll be damned," I said.

"We had a little short scene together. Like I was a teenager and you were showing me how to make a sailboat. That's how I remember your hands."

"A sailboat—oh, yeah," I said. Giddy with fatigue, I started repeating words tonelessly: "sailboat . . . mousey hair . . . Westport . . . braces . . . . "

"And here we are again," said Jennifer. "It's a groove."

"Yes," I said, slumping.

Hal, the producer, came to the door. "Jennifer, they want you in Wardrobe," he said. Jennifer rose languidly from the couch.

"See you later, Steven," she said, disappearing. Stephanie, her makeup finished, climbed silently out of the chair.

"Well!" with a toss of her head. "Isn't it fun to meet old friends." And she was gone.

"OK, yo yo," said Carl, coming around his chair and yanking off my towel in one graceful move, "let's see what we can do with *you*."

I climbed painfully into the chair. Staring goonishly at me in the mirror was an unshelled snail with windburn.

"Jesus," said Carl, rummaging around in his makeup box, "what that face needs is some new miracle fabric! It's a good thing angel ass didn't get a good look at that kisser."

"She was an apprentice in Westport," I said.

"Yeah, I heard," Carl said, using an ice pack now on my face. "I heard that the producer saw her playing a sweet little nurse on *Marcus Welby, M.D.* so they had her in for this. From what I hear about this goody doctor she's playing, she must have come to the audition dressed as a nun."

After the ice pack Carl used an astringent, then a layer

of some gummy substance. Then a white base, then a darker, then two different powders. With an incredible assortment of sponges, brushes, and pencils—daubing, drawing, shading, blending—using line and color with consummate skill, Carl went slowly and surely about the business of creating a kind of mask of my original features.

"Good thing I remember what you look like, yo yo," he said, stepping back to appraise his handiwork, then springing back to it. My lips, which had resembled something that might stare up at you out of a bowl of won ton soup, were being contoured into a literal creation of a human mouth. The exit-sign light under my forehead became a nose again. He was fantastic.

"Just don't smile too much," cautioned Carl sardonically, and waved me out of the chair.

Haltingly, I made my way downstairs to the rehearsal hall. Since my action involved standing in one spot in Act IV, and sitting throughout Act V, I survived the blocking rehearsal with a minimum of wear and tear. Jennifer Dryden, by the way, was coolly and calmly letter perfect in her words. If she was feeling any first-day jitters they were well hidden—which is more than could be said for the rest of her.

With help from Kate I struggled into my doctor's whites and, gripping the stairway banister like a hernia patient, propelled myself up the two flights to the studio.

Jennifer was standing nonchalantly among a group of stunned cameramen and crew. Even in a formless doctor's coat, Peter Pan collar, her blond hair tied up in a severe little bun and no makeup, she was managing to stop traffic. They were all introducing themselves to her and joshing about having various pains and could she help them.

"What a cute group," she said, turning toward me languorously. "Hey, you look groovy!"

In our fourth-act scene, Dr. Susan Williams appeared in Dr. Nevins's office to inquire about a patient of hers on whom I had recently operated. Toward the end of the scene I appeared, having been called by Dr. Nevins to confer with them.

                        Nevins
Dr. Cross, I thought you might be interested in this prog-
ress report on that trichotomy—Mr. Shuman in 312. Oh
(*Indicating Susan*), you know Dr. Williams, of course.
                        Harlan
Of course.
                        Susan
(*With a pleasant smile*) Hello, doctor.
                        Nevins
There are some interesting complications, apparently. I
think it might be worthwhile for you and Dr. Williams to
discuss the case with each other in some detail. I would
then like a follow-up report as soon as possible.
                        Harlan
Of course.
                        Nevins
Perhaps at lunch. (*Smiling*) The food in our cafeteria
should not distract you from serious matters.
                        Susan
Thank you, doctor.

   By air time, the day had become unreal for me. I had
fallen asleep twice: the first time over a half-eaten cheese-
burger in my dressing room, and then during notes after
dress rehearsal. As the day wore on, it became harder and
harder to connect myself to the hum of activity. It simply
seemed to be going on *around* me, as if I were still sitting
in the dressing room with the towel around my face. All
those odd, urgent sounds; the to-and-fro shuffling; the
nervous discussions; all those funny people running
around. Who was that little man running upstairs with
the space shoes and the clipboard? I wanted my towel
back.
   Court, the stage manager, was calling "Five minutes to
air." We straggled into the studio. There was organ music.
Court cueing people. Scenes being played.
   Act IV came up. Court cued me, I knocked on the
door, stood by the desk, and said "Of course," twice. So

far so good. I moved dreamily to the next set for Act V—the cafeteria chat with Dr. Williams. Now, even in the best of circumstances, cafeterias and restaurants are among the least favorite places to play scenes in. They abound in odd distractions: music, food, waiters, and worst of all, other diners—understandably bored extras who carry on animated real-life conversations all around you, accompanied by appropriate head bobbings.

I began by pulling Jennifer's chair out for her and neglecting to help her push it back, so that when she leaned toward me at the table, she looked as if she were lining up a difficult pool shot. I followed that by forgetting to pour her coffee, handing her an empty saucer instead. "Coffee?" I said blandly, handing her this plate.

Jennifer looked at me quizzically, the hint of a smile playing briefly across her face. I remembered the smile—the makeup room—no, before that—yes—yes of course—it was coming back to me now: the sailboat scene . . . Westport . . . braces.

"Well, Dr. Williams," I said, swatting images away like flies, "tell me about your patient's symptoms."

Jennifer began answering in a shy, serious, Dr. Williams voice. Having pulled her chair in deftly, she sat perkily upright now, her chest straining prettily against the lapels of her Dr. Williams coat. Fighting off memories of the beige see-through net, I looked over her shoulder to where a couple I had never seen before were taking seats at a table. Who were they? What had it looked like when I handed Jennifer that plate?

However manfully I strove to concentrate on Dr. Susan Williams and Mr. Shuman's trichotomy, astonished pauses began to precede my responses as my attention wandered fitfully from one distraction to the other. Now I was getting caught up in a spirited private conversation to our right about pets. In a rising and falling sotto voce, one of the extras was going on feverishly about a marvelous beagle he had. I found myself leaning precariously to my left trying to tune out on him.

During a crucial exchange in our scene, the dog man reached an emotion-charged section of his narrative about the beagle getting lost on Riverside Drive. I was in the middle of a rambling speech which summed up my impressions of Pinewood Hospital and which contained a lot of names.

" . . . so you see, San . . . Susan, I have always found Dicter Nuven . . . Doctor Nevin . . . I have always found Dr. Nevins . . . . " (What?)

(" . . . so I said to the cop, 'Listen, officer, my dog has been missing for three hours.' 'What's he look like?' says the cop . . . . ")

"I have always found Dr. Nevins a fair man to work with . . . for . . . . "

(" . . . dog jumped aboard somebody's Chris-Craft in the yacht basin . . . . ")

" . . . a brilliant man in the field, and of course, Ian is a . . . was one . . . is one . . . . " (What?)

(" . . . kept calling his name . . . 'Skippie! . . . here, Skipper! . . . .'")

"Ian is . . . and Paul Markham . . . . "

("The boat started moving! . . . . ")

"Paul and Nancy . . . Ian . . . . "

("I ran down the pier calling, 'Skippie! Skippie!'")

With a throaty, half-suppressed giggle, Jennifer looked up from behind her napkin and jumped on to her next speech. Behind her, the unknown couple were getting up from their table. The girl was blushing. I stared into Jennifer's eyes, wondering why the girl had blushed like that and how the dog man had got his beagle back.

Suddenly it hit me that momentarily Dr. Susan Williams would remark on how quickly I had finished my sandwich and ask if I would like some of hers. I hadn't touched the damn thing, what with the dog man and the blush girl. I jammed half the sandwich in my mouth and the other half into my pocket. Susan was asking me something.

"What time do you think you'll be able to look in on Mr. Shuman this afternoon?"

Strands of ham gristle were winding around my larynx. American cheese inundated my gums like a boxer's mouthpiece.

"I, ah, rr . . . gruuu . . . cerrrgufff!" I said, nodding furiously and holding up two fingers.

"Did you say two o'clock?"

"Yachht . . . uug tock," I sputtered.

"And you'll come by my office afterwards?" she went on coolly.

"Yachht . . . cerff."

"Thank you, doctor, and thanks so much for lunch. It's been lovely."

"Gruuuff."

Two weeks before, such a series of idiocies would have had me pacing and flailing and cursing myself around the studio like a maddened dervish. But now a vague and exhausted lack of ease was about the most dynamic feeling I could conjure up. I shambled toward my dressing room and dropped into the nearest chair.

There was an immediate knock on the door, followed by Jennifer Dryden, her Gucci bag in one hand and Cyrano in the other.

"That was kind of a groove," she said laughing indolently, depositing the bag and Cyrano on the cot and sitting in the chair next to me, hitching her skirt and crossing her long, strong legs. "Hey, you look really beat."

"Really?" I mumbled, turning toward the mirror over my dressing table and staring at Carl's Steven Prince mask.

"The heat in there is a drag," she added, pulling the zipper of her white Peter Pan jumper down to the navel.

"They turn off the air conditioning after the dress rehearsal," I said, trying not to notice in the mirror, as I began to wipe off my mask, that above Jennifer Dryden's navel there was a rib cage, and above that two glowing masses of pink flesh pushing through the billowed jumper.

"Because of the noise," I said, blinking.

"What?" she said, stretching over to the Gucci bag and pulling out some knitting.

"They turn off the air conditioning because of the noise," I repeated. My mirror: a split screen. On one side a half-naked girl knitting angelically, and dead ahead my bloated windburned face re-emerging with each swipe of Kleenex. The images merged and blurred. I was feeling a little faint.

"Hey, you don't look so good," she said. "Here." She leaned her chair backwards toward the cot and began rummaging through the Gucci bag again, coming up with a bottle of tiny green pills.

"Take one of these."

"What are they?"

"Peps."

"Peps?"

"Take one."

"No, no," I said. "I'll get some more tea from Frances."

"Who's Frances?"

"Frances Foy," I said. "She makes very good herb teas."

"Oh, yeah?" Jennifer was standing over me now, a meadow of soft flesh holding out two little green pills.

"She gives them to people—different teas," I mumbled.

"Take these pills," said Jennifer.

"OK," I said, popping the pills into the back of my throat and half standing to struggle out of my jacket.

"Which one is Frances?" said Jennifer, putting a cool hand on my forehead. "The one with the curlers?" A lemony skin smell wafted down at me.

"No, that's Stephanie," I said, falling back into my chair.

"I never remember names," she said, going back to her knitting. "I remembered you, though, right?"

"That's right, yes," I said.

"I never could forget you. You were cool in that play we did. I thought you were the best-looking guy I'd ever seen."

"Is that right?" I said. "That's very nice."

"You're still pretty groovy," she added simply. "How do you feel now?"

"Better," I said.

"Those pills are the greatest," said Jennifer.

"What's that you're knitting?" I asked.

"Like a bikini," she said, "for this guy I know." She stood up again, lifting her skirt up over her waist and holding a roughly 5″ x 6″ bit of red wool over her own black lace bikini pants. Fragments of soft pink flesh leaped out at me.

"Of course, it's not finished or anything," she said, moving her legs around.

"No—right—yes!" I said.

"But don't you think it's groovy?" Little black frills peeked around the edges of the red wool.

"Yes it is," I said, swallowing and managing a smile. "You say that's for a guy?"

"Yeah," she said, pulling the wool tighter.

"What kind of a guy? A real guy? A big guy?" I started to feel a little giddy.

"Yeah," she said, sitting again, "a guy I made this movie with."

"Is that what you've been doing since Westport—making movies?"

"And some TV. I lived out in Hollywood for three years and made five movies. Movies are a groove."

"What kind of movies?" I asked chattily.

"Two science fiction, a horror, and two like—you know, underground art flicks. This last one was where I met this guy."

"The bikini guy?"

"Yeah. We had this really neat nude swimming scene. I mean, you know—smooth—just, you know, real free and groovy. We made it under this waterfall." She stood up to illustrate. "And like this water kept knocking us up and down and pushing us into this small like grotto or cove or something, and I kept pushing against all this water." Jennifer lifted her arms, arching her back, her breasts falling free of the Peter Pan jumper, and spread her legs, acting out all the pushing up and down—"Pushing and falling back!" she said, tumbling suddenly onto the cot and pretending to be swimming. "And then we found this spot where we could kind of balance ourselves . . . ."

Something was happening to me—a kind of whirl. Suddenly there were two Jennifers, then three—fragmenting images—a Picasso mural: one round breast, one pink thigh, long blond hair falling down over two foreheads, a triangle of blue eyes . . . all moving crazily from the cot back to the chair . . . she was sitting down to her knitting again.

"But there were some really like, you know, kooky guys making that picture. They figured, you know, I mean—wow!—easy or something. But like I don't dig that stuff."

"Of course not," I said, trying to draw a bead on several fragments of black bikini swimming toward me.

"These two guys like got me down under the water—one of them holding me, and the other one . . . ."

Four strong, long legs floated by me and started moving toward the ceiling.

"This other one started trying to make out with me under the water . . . ."

Two pink navels undulating . . . .

"Hey, are you OK?" Three Jennifers rising and floating toward me, pink-frosted lips sinking into my bloated, windburned face . . . .

"Just a little dizzy," I braved.

"I guess I'd better split," she said. "You look really beat. Sure you're OK?" she asked, leaning down, touching my hand, then placing her hand over mine snugly. I stared down at her hand covering mine and wondered if she might bother to zip back up before wandering out into the hall.

"Real groovy hands," she said softly, zipping up and collecting her things. With Cyrano and the Gucci bag in tow, she turned in the doorway.

"See you tomorrow, right?"

"Right," I said.

She was gone. I stared dizzily into the mirror at a collage of red, swollen features. Residual visions of Jennifer Dryden danced in the mirror.

Changing back into street clothes involved a St. Vitus dance featuring stubborn trouser bottoms. Flailing and hopping, I finally managed the pants and was lurching toward my locker for my shirt when Frances Foy knocked and entered.

"I waited," she said.

"Oh?" I said, tucking and buttoning.

"For your apprentice friend to leave," she concluded archly.

"Apprentice friend?" The room was spinning.

"Miss Dryden."

"Oh, yeah," I said. "She gave me some pills."

"Pills? What kind of pills?" asked Frances quickly.

"Little green ones," I said, steadying myself on my dressing table.

"I've called Angela," said Frances, "and told her you're all right. And Tom is out getting a taxi."

"Angela? Taxi?"

"And Gustav is coming by to take you downstairs," she concluded, handing me my tie. Was I that bad? I looked in the mirror. Yes.

Claire, the front-desk receptionist, looked openmouthed as Gustav and I hurtled past her.

"Mr. Prince is recovering from a very serious vacation," explained Gustav, dragging me through the front door.

The advent of Jennifer Dryden created an initial furore around Studio 31. Word also spread throughout the Network Television Center itself that a child of nature had been loosed on the world of daytime TV. Actors from other shows began popping into our studio during rehearsals. Large guards with guns and dark glasses began showing up with messages usually delivered by phone. Jennifer, rehearsing, quickly became a tourist attraction.

Gustav acted as informal guide.

"Now, of course, she has to be in costume," he was pointing out to Willy, the massive guard who had rescued me months before on my first day on the show. (I hadn't seen him in our building since.)

"It's a pity she has to be so dressed," Gustav went on soberly; "usually she wears very little. Of course, in her Dr. Williams outfit, one cannot really appreciate. Her hair, for example, is actually long and silky, and her figure . . . of course now with that long, dreary coat . . . but her legs . . . fantastic . . . fantastic girl!" Willy chewed on his roast beef sandwich and nodded.

In fact, the contrast between Jennifer as Dr. Susan

Williams and Jennifer as Jennifer was mind boggling. The baby puma voice was modified to a sweet soprano, the open, insouciant manner transcribed itself into almost supernatural innocence, and her body, normally thrusting and languid, gathered itself primly under various loose-fitting doctor's garbs and modest knee-length frocks.

"Yeah, she's *nice* all right," said Willy, understating coolly.

Jennifer had finished the scene and was heading toward them to her dressing room. Gustav bowed and introduced Willy.

"What'cha got there?" she asked Willy, steadying herself on Gustav's shoulder to fix the flap on her shoe.

"Roast beef," Willy said, staring awfully.

"How about a bite?" she said. "I'm like starving." Soundlessly, Willy offered the sandwich. She leaned over, one hand still on Gustav's shoulder, and bit generously into the sandwich.

"Thanks," she said, turning away and flipping off through the door.

"Fantastic girl!" repeated Gustav.

"God—dam!" whispered Willy slowly, his jaw slack.

For her part, Frances Foy somewhat warily described herself as delighted "to have such an interesting new person on the show."

"Such an unusual girl, isn't she, Steven?"

"Yes," I said.

"And my goodness, so—ah—*attractive,* wouldn't you say?"

"Yes, yes," I said.

Frances and I were sitting in the set of Ruth and Phil Markham's living room. The Markhams were inviting Harlan over for dinner as a belated gesture of sympathy for his death in the family. Everyone was seeing Harlan now as a changed man. (Two weeks before, I'd been trying to steal her son's wife.) In fact this first week back was a crash course in moral regeneration for Harlan Cross. When I wasn't fixing up lymph glands, dispensing words of quiet wisdom to interns, or going to sympathy dinners, I was gently familiarizing myself with quiet and shy Dr.

Susan Williams. I was a good guy now, looking for a good girl.

"It's interesting," continued Frances, "that you should have known her before—in Westport, wasn't it?"

"Yes. She was much younger then," I said, "and smaller —pudgy."

"Pudgy?"

"Braces on her teeth and everything."

"And now you're going to have a romance with her on the show. So interesting. You know you're going to be *so* attractive as a good person—as Harlan I mean. Not that you weren't before—but in a different way, you know. And I think Miss Dryden is going to be with us for a long while."

"Really?"

"Oh, yes," she said knowingly.

Years of being a "good person" hovered stoically in my mind's eye. Good old Harlan, a thousand lymph glands later, graying at the temples, helping with the lawn.

"You know, Steven, you still seem done in from that odd vacation of yours." That was true. As the old Harlan Cross, I had been as tense as a coiled spring—antically alive: prowling, joking, bursting with nervous energy. Now? I felt as if I were wandering around in a field of poppies— sitting, lying, leaning against things. Just last night I had passed out on the shoulder of a dinner guest. And this morning again in the middle of shaving. Angela had discovered me crumpled backwards onto the clothes hamper in the bathroom, snoring happily, my face fully lathered— looking like a vanilla jelly apple with a carved smile. It had been almost a week since the horticulture ladies. What was happening?

"But I'm sure Jennifer Dryden will revive you," added Frances with a naughty twinkle.

I shuffled off to my dressing room wondering: old Harlan—good person. The former scourge of Middletown a benign figure now—full of floppy grins and happy sounds. No more homebusting, no more assaults on nurses in my fiery red MG. What now? Dr. Susan Williams.

Jennifer. Somehow the two weren't one. It was lunchtime. I went to sleep on my cot.

Unlike Harlan's conquests of old, my relationship with Dr. Susan Williams began diffidently. In fact, it was only after a certain amount of shilly shally that I had actually gotten her to go out with me.

Act II

Fade In:
An elegant restaurant. Harlan and Susan have finished their dinner and are soon to be served their coffee. Her hair is worn in the same severe bun as in the hospital. Her dress, conservative and attractive. Her manner throughout is demure, almost diffident.

Harlan

Would you like a brandy?

Susan

Oh, thank you, no—such a busy day tomorrow. But please don't let me stop you.

Harlan

No, no—I'm fine.

Susan

(*After a pause*) What a lovely place! Do you come here often?

Harlan

Occasionally.

Susan

(*After a pause*) I never did get to tell you how impressed I was with your follow-up diagnosis on Mr. Shuman. That occlusion between the sinoauricular node and the ventricles! Really amazing development.

Harlan

Yes. What made you get interested in medicine?

Susan

My father was a GP in our home town.

Harlan

Where was that?

Alexandria, Virginia. From the time I was very young, I loved to sit by myself in his library, poring over medical books. I loved to read. And I would get him to tell me all about the work he did. I always knew I wanted to be a doctor.

Harlan

What do you do in your spare time?

Susan

There doesn't seem to *be* very much. I have free clinic two nights a week. And keeping up with new developments in the field seems to take more and more time. I also help look after an aunt who lives here in Middletown.

Harlan

I see. What about recreation?

Susan

Recreation? Well, I like to listen to music, read—biographies mostly.

Harlan

There's a concert next Tuesday. The Detroit Symphony is in town. Would you like to go?

Susan

Oh, dear—Tuesday is free clinic. I'm sorry.

Harlan

There'll be other concerts.
(*Waiter brings coffee*)

Susan

Thank you. I must say, you're very different from what I expected.

Harlan

Am I?

Susan

You know how stories get around hospitals. And so many of them were about you.

Harlan

Sometimes things happen to change your perspective. Certain things that seemed important to me before don't seem so important to me now. In a strange way, life looks different to me.

Susan
(*Realizing he is alluding to his recent loss. But too shy to speak of it*) Yes. Yes, I know. I know what you mean . . . .

In the old days, we would have finished off the evening in her apartment. But this was a whole new ball game. This was a girl with free clinics and old aunts and high scruples, whose idea of a racy evening was to sit listening to Bach and poring over books on coronary occlusions. And how about the new Harlan! All that deference—the chastened manner.

The scene over, I trudged downstairs to my dressing room. This time Jennifer was already inside.

"Hi," she said.

"It's you," I said, throwing off my jacket and lumbering straight to the dressing table, without looking at her, to take off my makeup.

"Hey, guess what?" said Jennifer. "A pipe busted in my room and the floor's all flooded. You mind if I change in here?"

"Change?" I said, jumping up, then riveted by the soft metallic purr of her zipper. I sidled to the sink and began splashing cold water over my face.

"It's a real gas playing this chick, Susan." Between puma sounds there was the hushed rustle of silk.

"Kinda cute," continued Jennifer, "all that jazz about reading biographies and poring over medical books and stuff."

"You're good in the part," I said, making a big thing out of splashing my face.

"What?" she said.

I turned tentatively after what seemed enough time. "I said you're . . . . " I caught her, her head down, tying a mauve silk midriff snugly over her chest. Below the little bow there was nothing but bare skin and black bikini.

"Good in the part," I mumbled, turning back to the sink for more splashing.

"You wouldn't kid me, would you?" she said.

"No . . . listen, you know, if there's ever another flood or anything," I said, splashing a lot, "you *could* change in the ladies' room, maybe."

"With a lot of chicks running in and out?" said Jennifer, making more silk sounds.

"Of course there *is* that, yes," I conceded. "On the other hand, they might run in here too." I turned again, reaching for my towel on the chair. The backs of two long legs leading up to two black frills leaped out at me as Jennifer leaned over the Gucci bag, bringing out matching mauve hip huggers. The thought of anyone running into the room at that moment was dizzying. There was even less to the back part of the black bikini pants than there was to the front. "You never seem to have any clothes on in here," I said. Jennifer turned and wriggled into the matching mauve hip huggers.

"Cool," she said, buttoning up. "Hey, no kidding—you think I'm good in the part?" she said suddenly.

"Yes," I said, staring inadvertently at her bare midriff.

"I mean like acting is—you know—I just do it, you know? I mean it's fun sitting rappin' with you like we were these two other people."

"Yes," I said, looking up.

"But like I don't really know what I'm doing or anything." She struck a pose. "Hey, how do you like this gig? Groovy?"

"Very groovy," I said, wondering where to focus.

"You too," she said, then grabbed her Gucci bag and headed for the door. "Hey, you want a lift?" she asked suddenly.

"Lift?"

"Where's your pad?"

"Midtown," I said.

"Come on," she said, "this guy is downstairs waiting for me."

"The bikini guy?"

"No, some other guy. Come on."

"Thanks, but I'll get a cab."

"Aw, come on," she said, swooping up my coat and hustling me out the door. We were in the street. Halfway down the block a small red Triumph convertible, a huge head of hair behind the wheel.

"I'll get a cab," I repeated. "There's not enough room in there."

"C'mon," she said, grabbing my arm and presenting me to "Chip."

"Chip, this is Steven," she said. Chip looked up and grinned. Tan and hairy, wearing a tank top, leather jacket and bell bottoms, he swung around and opened the door.

"What's up?" he said.

"Lift to midtown," she said.

"Let's make it, I'm late," he said, revving the motor.

"How do we do this?" I said, indicating the two bucket seats.

"I'll use your lap," said Jennifer. "Go on."

"Let's move it," said Chip. I jumped in, Jennifer climbing in on top of me, and we roared away from the curb.

"Ahhh!" shouted Jennifer, arching her back and leaning into the wind, her hands behind her gripping my hips to balance. Chip gunned the car around the first corner without braking.

"Hold on!" I yelled, grabbing her as she leaned out against the curve. As the car straightened and shot ahead down the avenue I noticed my left hand seemed wedged into her bare midriff, and my chin was tucked under her ear—her hair whipping about my face.

"How ya doin', Dad?" said Chip, leaning across us to the dashboard for cigarettes as we stopped for a red light.

"Dad?" I said, trying to find an appropriate place for my right hand now as Jennifer swiveled around on my lap to light his cigarette. The car shot forward. Over Jennifer's mauve shoulder a stunned little Oriental guy with a shopping cart leaped backward out of our path, his face frozen into a stoic grimace.

"Chip does commercials," Jennifer said, swiveling back into me. She lifted the cigarette from between Chip's white teeth, took a languid drag on it, and returned the pinked tip to his mouth. "You know that one with the surfers—for that hair lotion? Chip's the tall one with the groovy bod."

Chip's groovy bod was leaning perilously to the left now. He had crossed lanes to cut off a delivery truck, and a herd of taxis were bearing down on us. He veered crazily and roared through a corner gas station—threading his way through gas pumps, parked cars, and two astonished attendants, breaking out into a side street, then screeching and spinning back onto the avenue—the two entrance bells pinging in mad succession behind us.

With Jennifer wrapped convulsively around me I reached up through a sea of flesh, barking inarticulate commands to stop the car. We screeched to a halt.

"This you?" asked Chip laconically, staring through blue-tinted glasses at the doorway of a pawnshop.

"Close enough," I mumbled, as Jennifer slid over onto his lap, tucking her legs up onto the steering wheel. I wrestled out of my seat, barely hitting the curb as the motor screamed again and they roared off, the open door swinging wildly and Jennifer still in Chip's lap, waving goodby.

Shaken, I walked the rest of the way home. Angela greeted me at the door.

"I caught the scene today. That new girl is very sweet."

"Sweet!" I said, still shaking. "Are you kidding? Crazy! I was almost killed just now!"

"What?" said Angela.

"This crazy girl insisted on giving me a lift with her crazy boyfriend!"

"What was wrong with that?"

"Wrong with it? It was incredible! *She's* incredible! Comes in my room. In there when I get there. I was tired. I wanted to sit down—rest. Forget it. *She's* in there—talking and rolling around."

"Rolling around?"

"Well, *running* around—you know—incredibly—*animated*. When you're tired like that—distracting. The other day too."

"She came in your room the other day too?"

"Yeah."

"For what?"

"I don't know—telling stories—these crazy stories about making movies and stuff."

"I think you're just tired," said Angela.

"You haven't *seen* her!"

"I saw her on the show; she looks very nice."

"On the *show*—that's *different*. She's not like that. That's acting. She's wild. The place is in an uproar around there. Guards coming in to watch her rehearse, strange people following her down the halls, crazy boyfriends!"

"Maybe," said Angela, "that guy who drove you was just someone she knew."

"Oh, no! Are you kidding? Groovy bod? The way she looked at him. Smoked his cigarette? I saw the way she looked at him. And you ought to see the clothes she wears! Unbelievable! All see through, and peek through—pink skin—nothing underneath."

"How do you know?"

"What?"

"How do you know there's nothing underneath?"

"You can *tell*—I mean with the see through, you know. Incredible! Do you know what this guy called me?"

"Who?"

"Groovy bod."

"What?"

"Dad! DAD!"

"Why are you so excited about it?" Angela asked suddenly.

"Excited? I'm not excited!"

"It doesn't seem important."

"I didn't say it was important. It's crazy. I was just almost killed, for example."

"Come sit and rest," said Angela.

"She's not safe with that hop head, that speed freak! For all I know, she could be dead right now!"

Angela looked up after a pause. "Nothing underneath, huh?" she said.

"Son of a bitch calling me 'Dad'! I'll break his head!"

"What do you mean she was rolling around your room?" said Angela.

"What?"

"Why was she rolling around your room?"

"Not rolling," I said. "Running."

"Why *your* room?"

"*Her* room was flooded. I told you that."

"Well, why didn't she run around Tom's room or Gustav's room? Why *your* room—with nothing underneath?"

"I don't know. Her scenes are with me for one thing. And she remembered me from Westport."

"Westport?" said Angela quickly.

"Yeah. She was an apprentice in Westport when I was there with *One for the Road.*"

"Oh, really?"

"Pudgy kid—braces . . . . "

"But you remembered her," said Angela.

"Not right away. Later. Later I remembered."

"You mean," suggested Angela, "when she was rolling around your room? There's a certain way she has of rolling around that you remembered?"

"No, no—don't be silly," I said. "I remembered because of this scene she mentioned—with the sailboat."

"Sailboat?"

"Yes. She remembered my hands fixing this sailboat."

"Your hands?"

"Yeah."

"Well, I do think it's a little strange," said Angela, moving toward the kitchen briskly, "a girl just coming on the show and running around men's rooms with nothing on underneath. Remembering men's hands. She was in Westport, huh?"

"Actually, that description is out of context," I said pursuing her. "She doesn't spend all her time running around rooms, and she does wear *something* underneath. It's not as if she were literally naked."

"How do you know?"

"What?"

"How do you know she wears something underneath?"

"Well, she'd *have* to, wouldn't she? I mean what with bending and everything."

"She does a lot of bending," said Angela. "You were conscious of a lot of bending," she went on in a flat, matter-of-fact voice. "So this crazy girl who knew you in Westport does a lot of bending—besides all the rolling around."

"Look," I said, "she's not *actually* crazy. I shouldn't have said that. She's really . . . . "

"Good," said Angela, closing the subject. "I'm glad she's not actually crazy. Shall we eat?"

Speculation concerning what Jennifer Dryden wore underneath was not confined to the home by any means. There were in-depth discussions around the studio as well, along with daily reviews of the see throughs, hip huggers, midriffs, and micro minis. It inspired people in different odd ways. Stephanie, for example, cut her hair. Tom Curtis found a new vigor. And Gustav, as might be expected, was in a fairly constant state of euphoria.

Frances Foy, however, was moved to recall the past. "Imagine a young woman walking around like that in broad daylight. It's unbelievable," she said. "I think what's missing in the way girls look today," she went on, "is elegance. When I was a girl, we had style. Patou, Mainbocher, Schiaparelli—designed such beautiful clothes for us. Works of art! I remember when I was in *Charlot's Review* with Gertrude Lawrence in 1924, Baron De Meyer did my portrait. I wore a lovely Fortuny gown—all pleated and sculpted and a little fur-edged gold chiffon lame wrap. Breathtaking! We had *style!* Marion Morehouse, and Tilly Losch and Eleanore Belmont—*they* were great beauties—so elegant!

"I'll never forget, I was at a party at Hartley Manners' and Laurette Taylor's place on Riverside Drive. Such a grand old place. Barrymore was there and Gladys Cooper and, oh, so *many* interesting people. I was very young and shy, standing alone by the fireplace. And Mrs. Belmont came over to me and introduced herself. She took my hand and said, 'My dear, you have such true elegance.

What is your name?' *Well*, it was just about the most wonderful thing anyone had ever said to me!"

Court's voice interrupted. "Places please for Act III—the Markham kitchen. This is a two-set scene, and remember there's a cake in the oven, so no stomping."

"Oh, that's me," said Frances, standing and moving toward the door. "Well, dear Steven, my point is these girls leave nothing—absolutely nothing—to a poor man's imagination. And the use of a man's imagination is one of the most powerful weapons a woman has. Don't you agree?"

"A man's imagination?" I said. "Yes, yes—I agree—absolutely."

SIX

Writers of daytime serials could rightfully point to each other with pride as being among the miracles of human endurance. That is if they were able to uncrook their typing fingers after writing three thousand five hundred words a day five days a week. Just churning out your own name three thousand five hundred times a day would be tough. But imagine creating dialogue that makes sense at that rate: words that keep plot developments humming—and that sound right—coming out of the mouths of fifteen or so different characters, all of whom have different problems and their own way of thinking and reacting. (To say nothing of having different-shaped mouths.) And who are portrayed by actors of assorted temperaments, qualities, voices, looks, and ages.

And having to consider, while they are juggling four or five concurrent story lines, which ones are working best? Which should be emphasized? Which relegated to limbo? To oblivion? And which characters are registering best with the audience?

Odd chain reactions are often forged from such reflections. A bad girl may be brought in to get a married good guy into trouble and become an unexpectedly quick favorite with the audience. Parents are invented for her;

a terrible experience traumatizes her into decency; and she winds up marrying someone else on the show. In six months she and the original lover are acknowledging each other with polite little smiles as if the recent past were a figment of the imagination. Or the hastily improvised parents may ring the bell and the girl be shunted off into obscurity. It's entirely possible to come on as a potential murderer and wind up mayor of the town.

Besides keeping fifteen characters in varying degrees of flux with assorted heartbreaks, illnesses, misunderstandings, unrequited loves and thwarted strivings, there are the emergency situations for which logical absences, disappearances, and deaths have to be improvised: an actress playing somebody's fiance gets pregnant in real life. How long can she be shot from the chest up, smiling seraphically from poufs and couches? And then what? Or an actor takes a leave of absence to do a play, and when he returns has to be written out for Wednesday matinees. There are vacations to account for. And finally there are the actors who decide to leave the show at the ends of contracts.

As if all of this were not enough to keep the writers on their toes, there is the matter of keeping the audience totally abreast of the story. It has to be assumed that even the most faithful watchers may miss one day or days in a given week through some scheduling lapse: a sudden illness perhaps, or a death in the family, or some carelessness or other, and miss a pertinent plot fact. Daily episodes must therefore contain summaries of days previous. Such a line as, "You knew, of course, that Marge and Dave are planning to visit Dave's folks, but they haven't told Jimmy," may seem unpregnant to some, but to those people who missed last Tuesday's show, it is a link, a small corner piece in the total mosaic.

Most serial writers work in teams, presumably so that when one collapses the other can keep going, or call the doctor, or so that if one of them comes up with a good idea in the middle of a catatonic seizure the other one can write it down.

Not wanting to leave a stone unturned, our writers

decided to strengthen Harlan Cross's new image as a good guy by investing him with a parent. It wasn't enough, apparently, to have a good girlfriend. I was now to have a mom.

I imagined one of the writers shaking the other awake in the middle of the night—trembling with excitement and large with idea.

"George, I think it's happening!"

"What?"

"Harlan has a mother."

"God, that's wonderful! When?"

"Soon, I think."

"Oh, that's marvelous. My God! Why are you on your hands and knees cleaning the floor like that? You should be resting!"

"No, no—I feel like it. I'll just tell you the rest of it while I'm finishing up. Then you can call."

"Anything you say."

"Well, here it is. She's coming back from Europe because her husband who's an army colonel stationed in Brussels has died."

"I get it. A death in the family."

"That's right, George. And now she's coming to Middletown to be with her son until her affairs are straightened out and she gets her peace of mind back."

"I get it. She becomes jealous of Harlan's feelings for Dr. Susan Williams."

"Right, George."

"There's a battle for Harlan's affections between his mother and Susan."

"Right!"

"What will we call her?"

"Grace."

"Wonderful! Hey, as long as you're still on your knees— you missed a spot over there in the corner."

I dropped into Frances Foy's dressing room to ask her if she had heard the news about my impending sonhood. She was way ahead of me.

"Not only are you going to have a mother, Steven dear,

but do you know *who* is playing her? I just heard it from Hal."

"Who?" I said.

"Naomi Talbot."

"Naomi Talbot! She's still alive?"

"Apparently," said Frances.

Naomi Talbot! What memories were conjured! Associations! Hadn't she been a special friend of Scott and Zelda Fitzgerald's? Won an Academy Award in a film with Gable? Hadn't she been, for a while, the toast of Broadway in plays by Philip Barry, Maxwell Anderson, and Robert Sherwood?

"In my day, Naomi Talbot was one of the great beauties," said Frances. "God! I'll never forget her! Tall and incredibly graceful—beautiful white skin and bright red hair. The way she took that stage! What presence! She had an indescribable quality—luminous."

"And now she's going to be my mother," I said, wondering.

There was a knock at the door. It was Gustav, wanting to use Frances's phone.

"Forgive me, Frances, my sweetheart, but all the other phones are tied up, and I have become involved in the newest Reiner household crisis. It has now to do with plumbing," said Gustav, picking up the phone and dialing. "Claire, the receptionist, just received a call for me from my neighbor's bathroom. Apparently my entire family is in my neighbor's bathroom, including the cat. My wife reminded me that I must call a Mr. Bellini, a plumber who hates to work and doesn't speak English very well.

"Hello, Mr. Bellini! This is Mr. Reiner—listen . . . what? . . . your wife? I am a favorite of your wife on television . . . that's wonderful. Perhaps then you would be kind enough to look at my septic tank that has exploded. Septic tank. You should know it quite well, you have already fixed it several times . . . yes . . . it exploded last night in the middle of a garden party. Quite distracting. I must say I thought of you as my guests ran to their cars, Mr. Bellini . . . . "

After much arguing and haranguing, Gustav put down the phone.

"The best thing about being on this show is that I can get out of my house when these terrible things keep happening to it."

"Have you heard the news?" said Frances. "Steven is going to have a mother."

"Of course I know he's going to have a mother," said Gustav with a wave of his hand. "Why not? After all, he's already had everyone else, so why not a mother?"

"Naomi Talbot," added Frances.

"Naomi Talbot!" The name stopped Gustav in his tracks. "My God! We did a play together once. What a woman! My God, she must be as old as I am!"

When Gustav gets into the spirit of a conversation he prowls—throwing his legs one in front of the other, then spinning around, weaving, bending forward and back, running his hands through his thick white hair, and gesticulating grandly. The mention of Naomi Talbot's name turned him into a dervish and unleashed a flood of reminiscences. Frances waded in with additions and corrections.

Three marriages . . . oil millionaire . . . South American cattle baron . . . romance with John Gilbert . . . legendary three-day parties . . . fortunes made and lost . . . .

"Yes," said Gustav, stopping in mid-prowl, "I did, I remember now absolutely."

"Did what?" queried Frances.

"Have actually a short affair with her at one time. In Hollywood—September . . . very hot in September. At the time I reminded her I believe of a hairy Erich Von Stroheim."

"What was it like?" I asked.

"Extremely humid. And marvelous!" said Gustav, spinning. "It was around that time also that a duel was fought over her by a famous director and a polo player."

"And now she's going to be your mother," said Frances, looking at me and shaking her head. "Isn't that something?"

Gustav looked too, standing crookedly—one leg wrapped around the other—and leaning backwards like a piece of comic sculpture.

Somehow the full implication had not till then borne in on me.

A legend! My mother?

Although other stars had already been coaxed out of variously inspired retirements and inactivities to join the swelling daytime TV ranks, the advent of Naomi Talbot was a special day for us, managing to upstage even Jennifer Dryden in the flurry-causing department.

She arrived at Studio 31 quietly late, in sweater and slacks, and without a retinue of any kind. First the eyes—luminous green, almond shaped, and lidded heavily, suggesting depths. They were set in a time-ravaged face constructed out of finely made bones, delicate and symmetrical, the kind of face once able to be captured beautifully at any angle but puffed now and wrinkled: an odd match to her still youngish, well-toned body.

Frances and Gustav greeted her warmly, Gustav bowing magnificently and kissing her hand, following which she sauntered through introductions to everyone and let out a loud, deep-throated laugh.

"First of all, I want you to know I watch you all every day out at the farm, and I don't know how the hell you do it! Where's the guy?"

For a moment we wondered who "the guy" was. It turned out to be our director, Max Brand.

"I'm in your hands, baby. Can you stand it?" she said, putting her arm in Max's and letting out another laugh—a sound that was a cross between the bark of a seal and a rush of rapids. "Let's talk," she said, leading Max toward the door. The rehearsal would be delayed for a bit.

I took a second cup of coffee and pondered. This legendary lady was going to be my mother! Grace Cross—a nice, protective American mom? In Middletown? Unbelievable!

Rehearsing our scene in Harlan's apartment, in which he and Grace talk a lot about Colonel Cross, Naomi Talbot went about getting the lines and blocking without trying any acting to speak of—mumbling her words and writing a lot of things in her script. Periodically there would be the ferocious, barking laugh followed by a question with a sharp point on it.

"How do I say that line without making them change channels?" she asked suddenly, looking at Max with a no-kidding grin. Heads turned. Hal, our producer, shot his hands skyward. "Ha ha!—Whoops, baby! Nami baby!" Hal tries to keep things light and easy with a kind of short-hand chatter, like a shortstop talking it up in the infield. His answer to tension is to speak in frenzied ellipses and to run around making sounds, and grinning, and patting people. He also stands around 6′ 3″, played football at Colgate and, if he wanted to pat you hard enough, could break your back.

"Did I say something wrong?" challenged Naomi.

"Shows you're thinkin'—beauty goin'—yes, Bob!" Hal was throwing his arms around like a sailor giving deck signals. Max was smiling masonically.

"Just say the line simply," suggested Max, looking at Naomi levelly.

"OK for you, old guy," said Naomi, not unpleasantly, "you're just sitting there with a lot of pencils. I'm the one who's got to make this dame work."

Max kept smiling.

"Oh ho! Yes! Babe—Nami, hon!" said Hal, rolling his eyes and rapping the table in an antic pantomime of a judge insisting on order in the court. People looked up from their coffee and smiled. I put my arm around Naomi's shoulder and smiled. (Since I spend most of the day without my glasses, I tend to smile at anything that moves.)

A discussion of the offending line led to a lengthy chat about the scene. Max was shooting looks at the clock. Each act is given roughly twenty-five minutes for discussion, blocking and running it through twice. Starting at 8 a.m., the director has to fit in these three steps before 10:00, when he must be on the floor for conferences with cameramen and audio men, check the sets, go over his floor plan with Andy, the lighting man, and complete other various details prescribed by the demands of the particular script. He's got to be through with that by 10:30 so he can begin to rehearse in the studio.

For all the smiling and pleasantry, the director is fighting time continually. My director friend O'Brian told me that he carries a clock around inside his head. That he knows what a minute and thirty-seven seconds is the way a man knows when he's falling in love. When you go to the fights with O'Brian, he always sits back in his seat just before the bell rings. There's a little "bing" inside his brain right at the three-minute mark.

Max Brand looked up at the clock, his smile broadening, and put his arm around Naomi Talbot's other shoulder. The three of us looked as if we were thinking up a play for touch football.

"I've got three more acts to do now," he said; "we'll get to it again in the studio." Naomi looked around. We were all smiling and nodding. The actors in the next scene were moving from their seats around the table, tables and chairs were shifted, Terry, the production assistant, was calling Frances Foy out of her dressing room. Everyone's clock was moving. I took Naomi's arm and suggested she might want to know where the makeup room was. Temporarily stilled, she suffered herself to be led down the hall. We ran into Kate, scuttling along with a wounded nurse's uniform over her arm, a mouthful of bobby pins, and various needles and threads streaming down her ample front.

"Sure is nice having you here with us, Miss Talbot," garbled Kate, her voice kazooing through the bobby pins. "You probably don't remember, but I dressed you once at the Blackstone Theater in Chicago."

"Of course," said Naomi Talbot nicely, staring at the pins.

"Your room is number four," said Kate, fishing around in her apron pocket for the right locker key. "Here's your key, and for God's sake, don't lose it!"

"Right—o," said Naomi.

"Steven'll show you the room," said Kate, disappearing down the hall.

I opened the door to number four and Naomi put her

coat and bag down on the dressing table and looked the room over quickly.

"A nice, functional little room," I said in my best bell-hop voice. "If you need anything, just ring the front desk and they'll ignore you totally."

"Where's the sunken bath?" asked Naomi, removing some nostrum things from her bag and lining them up on the dressing table.

"We only have those in the *eight*-dollar rooms," I said.

"Well, I guess this will do," she said with a throaty laugh.

"Will there be anything else?" I asked, bowing.

"Yes," she said. "Have you got a cigarette? I'm trying to quit—even tried one of those plastic pacifiers, but I kept lighting the goddam thing!" I gave her a cigarette. "My God!" she said, moving around the room and laughing again. "There was a time when they'd have had to use tear gas to smoke me out of that old house of mine. And here I am back in a dressing room again." Idly, she opened the closet door. Inside were a few torn operating gowns and a row of shoes for large orderlies.

"Oh," she said.

"Would you like to try on some shoes?" I said.

"I hope the styles are a little snappier in the eight-dol-lar rooms," she said, closing the door and moving back toward the mirror, squinting into it critically. "Who said 'when there's no more room for another crow's foot you attain a kind of peace'? Who said that? Some wise-ass."

I looked at the reflection in the mirror, remembering Naomi Talbot in the few films of hers I'd seen, and trying to distinguish the voice, the mannerisms, the tilt of her head when she listened, her particular smile.

"By the way," she said, "who's that blond number with the big boobs?"

"You mean Jennifer?"

"The one who looks like she should be coming up out of a cake."

"That's Jennifer," I said. "She's Dr. Susan Williams."

"You mean the mousey little doctor with the Bo-Peep voice?"

"Yeah," I said.

"She must wear a sandwich board under those Mary Jane blouses," continued Naomi, still staring at the mirror. "Well, hell, I didn't wear my first bra until I was fifty."

"Did you frame the label?" I said.

She put her head back and laughed, stopping suddenly at an announcement over the P.A. Terry's voice was paging me.

"What now?" asked Naomi, sitting up suddenly, prepared for the next uncertainty.

"I have to get back to the rehearsal room," I said. "I'll show you where makeup is, and then I'll see you later."

"Makeup?" she said quickly. "I do my own makeup." The words snapped out like a short drum roll.

"Not on TV," I said. "I mean—it's different."

"Oh, yeah?"

After running my Act IV scene in the rehearsal hall, I came back to the makeup room to see how Naomi Talbot was doing with Carl. When I walked into the room, Carl was making a point in a voice bristling with cool. At night he makes up opera divas at the Met. This was obviously his opera diva voice.

"Now, Miss Talbot, you are supposed to be in mourning. You are a *mother* in mourning. It says so right here," he said, holding out the cast breakdown sheet with both hands as if he were offering a plate of hors d'oeuvres. "You are Harlan's mother. Harlan is Steven—the yo yo standing behind you there with the glasses. That's your big son. You're his *mama*."

"I know I'm his mama!" said Naomi, her voice rising dangerously.

"You're Grace Cross, a woman in her sixties, still in shock from the death of her poor husband. You are tired from a long, exhausting trip."

"Balls!" said Naomi Talbot. "I'm an *actress*. This is theater. Theater with cameras."

"This is Middletown, Miss Talbot. And that Mata Hari eye shadow has got to go."

Under the hairdryer, Stephanie's face peered out attentively at the scene. I joined Pepe on the couch. There was a loin-girding pause.

"Now look, baby!" barked Naomi, sitting up straight in the makeup chair. The voice that had been so full of mellow chortles in her dressing room had honed to a fine cutting edge. "I know more about goddam makeup than Perc Westmore. I was an expert, baby, before you knew how to make mudpies in a sandbox!"

"It says Grace Cross, not Theda Bara!" said Carl, flicking at the breakdown sheet as if he were dusting it.

"Get this through your head, fella: I'm not going on looking like death eating a cracker!"

"But the cast breakdown . . . . "

"*Screw* the cast breakdown!" yelled Naomi. "Screw the goddam cast breakdown! Now hand over that eyebrow pencil before you hurt yourself with it."

She looked back at me. "I suppose we're supposed to *be* someplace now, aren't we?"

"Upstairs in five minutes," I said.

"I figured," she said, swinging her legs out of the chair. "Keep your sponges warm, baby," she said to Carl, and headed out of the room.

At the first camera run-through, strange things began happening to Naomi Talbot's performance. Although at first run-through you're usually too busy worrying about cameras and mikes and lines and moves to pay much attention to your partner, there was no escaping the fact that Grace Cross, my little old mom, was becoming a creature of fantasy before my very eyes. What were those odd new readings? The studied pauses long enough to let a parade through? Those mannerisms suddenly creeping up out of nowhere? The voice that kept gaining octaves?

A new Naomi Talbot was emerging, making it practically impossible to remember the one we had met earlier. Where was that salty old lady in slacks? The kidder with the whiskey-sour laugh? And who was this flapper in curls? This coquette with the inched-up skirt?

It was only after a few stops and starts that I began to realize what was going on. Naomi Talbot was turning on her own special version of the star!

"Harlan! Harrrlan! I can't *tell* you what it *meannns* . . . " (incredible pause, a sweeping look at the camera, then a lowering of eyes, a halfway glance) "to your mother, for *usss* to be . . . " (pause, slow building smile) "*together!* It's been so" (unbelievable pause, hand to forehead, quick look up at the camera, quick brave smile, eyes lowered suddenly, head brought slowly up) "*hard!*"

Mesmerized by all the sudden pantomiming, I had a hard time latching on to my cue. Had she said it? What? Is she finished?

"I know it has, Mother," I said, chancing it.

Max's voice broke through over the P.A.

"Naomi, dear. I'm intercutting here. And it's a little tough to know what's happening. I go from Harlan to you, and you're doing these *things,* and it's a little strange. Also we're losing time in the scene."

"Oh, really," said Naomi.

We started again. Harlan's longish speech about how often he'd thought of Grace and the colonel. Something new started to happen. All sorts of strange reactions punctuated my lines: sighs and gasps and body things.

"I've thought so many times, Mother (sigh) . . . of you and Father (gareoo?) . . . I know I've been pretty much (ahhhee?) . . . pretty much of a prodigal (eeahhh) and I . . . . "

Max again. "What's that? What are those noises? Is that a camera? Air conditioning? What?"

Naomi wore a strange look of total absorption. She didn't seem to hear Max's voice or to see me, or to be concerned with why the action had stopped. The only things that seemed "there" for her were herself and the cameras. She took the moment to dart out of the set and look through the viewfinder of number-one camera. Jimmy, the cameraman, stepped back openmouthed.

"Isn't there an awful lot of top lighting?" she said.

"What?" said Max over the P.A., still trying to figure

out what all Naomi's reaction sounds had been as events began speeding past him.

Andy, the lighting designer, rushed over. "We have to adjust from general lighting here," he explained levelly. "There isn't time for special setting up of every scene."

"Oh," said Naomi, "that's really too bad."

"What?" said Max, still waiting.

Near the prop table Eddie, the teleprompter engineer, was feeding corrected copy (cuts and changes) into the machines.

"What are those things?" asked Naomi, pointing.

"Teleprompters," said Court.

"What are *they* for?"

"They have all the lines on them in case anyone gets hung up," said Court easily.

"Hung up?" said Naomi. "We never use those in films. Lines! Lines! Everybody talking about lines. It's what's *under* the lines, darling. When you get *underneath*, into the *belly* of the scene, the lines are *there*, they *come*."

"I guess that's right," said Court, choosing his words. "It's just that with so little time for preparing . . . . "

"Time! Lines! Minutes!" said Naomi with a disdaining wave. "Steven, do you use them?"

"I can't even see them," I said.

"You see, Steven doesn't use them," she said, tapping Court's shoulder and walking back into the set.

"As long as we're stopped," said Naomi, speaking up at Max through the boom mike, "I'd like you to see another dress. This one I'm wearing has an awful lot of blue in it for this set." She waved toward Kate, standing in a corner with several alternate dresses over her arm.

"Now I think this beige would be lots better. Kate!" Kate hustled over, holding out a beige dress.

"We're not supposed to be stopped." Max's voice had risen perceptibly. "I've got three more acts to run here. Will someone tell me what those sounds were?"

Hal, the producer, was out on the floor now. "What's up, Nami, babe?" he said, wearing a big smile. Andy was whacking at an overhead light with his bamboo pole.

Court spoke up into the boom mike. "I think what you were hearing, Max, was Miss Talbot. Miss Talbot was reacting to Harlan there—sort of during his speech."

Naomi swung around, holding the beige dress up to her, modeling it for the camera.

"The beige is better," she stated.

"I think you're right," said Hal, stepping back inspectingly. "Nami roo bah! The beige is better. Max? Can you see the beige on her? Can you hear my heart?"

Court and I sat down on the couch. "Hey, Steven, I just heard I'm working the Kentucky Derby."

"Good thing," I said. "Louisville's a nice town and it's a lovely track." Court had taken off his headset, and I could hear Max squawking through it like an angry swan.

"But the skirt will have to be shortened," continued Naomi, striding around the set with the dress wrapped around her.

"What's the best hotel?" asked Court.

"The Brown," I answered.

Kate was making doubtful clucking noises. "I don't know if I'll have time," Kate said.

"What? What!" said Hal, running to her.

"I can't wear it unless the skirt is shortened," announced Naomi.

"We'll take care of it, Nami, babe!" said Hal, his Scotch-taped smile drooping.

Andy was shouting something up into the mike about the lights. Jimmy, the cameraman, sat down on the couch with Court and me and described a great hamburger he'd once had in Louisville.

"They put this special cole slaw and relish and mayonnaise on it."

"What?" said Hal, spinning toward him.

"Hamburgers in Louisville," I said, clarifying.

Max's voice fought through the babble. "Can we get going now!"

"From where?" I said.

"From Harlan's speech, 'I've thought so many times . . . .'"

The scene continued shakily—Naomi improvising freely, going up in her lines from time to time, and coming up with new and unexpected moves that had the cameras swooping around to follow her like so many confused dolphins.

Max was patience on a monument during notes.

"Naomi, the scene is way over. We need three minutes. I don't want to make any more cuts, but I'll have to if you don't close up some of those pauses."

"Everything is *minutes* here, isn't it," she said, standing in front of the mirror, hitching up her skirt. Kate was on her knees, pinning.

"Don't you think my hair still looks awfully frowsy?"

"No," said Max. "Now in the speech about Colonel Cross, you have to relate that more to Harlan. After all, you're talking about Harlan's father. I have a lot of two-shots in there and . . . . "

"I think my hair is too frowsy," repeated Naomi.

"And when you look away from him into the camera, it looks like a soliloquy or something."

"But it's a *reminiscence!*" said Naomi. "And anyway when I look at Harlan, I'm completely in profile."

"But I have head shots of you on camera one," persisted Max.

"Not too close, I hope," she said. "This makeup is so . . . *vague*. By the way, I've *had* it with death-mask Charley down there!"

"Grace is supposed to be in her sixties," said Max calmly.

"Yes, darling, but she doesn't have to look like Sam Jaffe in *Lost Horizon*, for God's sake!"

Despite Max's dogged efforts, it became obvious by the after-lunch run-through that Grace Cross—my poor old death-in-the-family mother, was going to emerge in front of twelve million people as a combination of Zelda Fitzgerald and Betty Boop. It was too late to stop Naomi now, and anyway she had spent the entire break between dress rehearsal and air wrangling with Pepe over her hair and fretting with Carl about her eyes.

"You've got me looking like a goddam fetus!" she roared, standing up in the makeup chair and leaning forward precipitately, slathering brown shadow back on her lids. She and Carl had been at each other most of the day. They were going into their final rounds and Carl wasn't pulling any punches.

"You're supposed to be his mother! M-O-T-H-E-R, MOTHER! Not his girlfriend! He's got a girlfriend!"

But it was hopeless. And getting late.

"Come on, Naomi," I said, "you look great. Let's run the scene."

She looked like one of those plaster-of-paris dolls made in Poland.

"I want to see if there's any powder in the powder room first," she said, stepping out of the chair defiantly. "I'll see you in a few minutes."

"All right," I said.

She walked out of the room and down the hall in her too young, too short beige dress, a profusion of neon red sausage curls spilling down over her forehead like the innards of a broken toy.

"Jesus!" breathed Max wearily, slapping his leg with his clipboard. He had just delivered ten solid minutes of notes to Naomi Talbot. She had listened to them with an unseeing, vacant look—now and then arguing, or evading, or simply pretending not to understand.

Frances Foy took me aside worriedly. "I tried saying a few things to her," said Frances, "but it's no use."

Jennifer Dryden joined us. "Is she really going to do all those like weird things? I mean on the air? Wow!"

Pepe was packing away his combs and pins and curlers like a prizefight trainer whose fighter has just been carried out of the ring. "Couldn't stop her!" he mumbled. "Can you believe those wispy curls!"

I paced the hall waiting for Naomi to come out of her powder room. Hal rushed by, wearing the expression of a man who's just been told that his house burned down.

"Where is she?" he said, spinning back toward me, his mind obviously crowded with terrible, unspoken possibilities.

"In the powder room."

"The *what?* Oh. Fantasidonknow," he said, starting one word, finishing with another, then running off.

Max Brand, with Terry on his heels drawing lines

through the notes he'd already given, came barreling out of the wardrobe room and down the hall toward me. Beads of perspiration stood out on his upper lip like sprinkles on an ice cream cone.

"Steven, we're two minutes over, and the time has got to be gained in your scene with her. I've cut the other scenes to the bone already. Help me, OK? She just doesn't seem to understand about the time or . . . . "

"OK," I said. Max sped away. "Or anything," he was on the verge of saying.

In a moment the ladies' room door opened and Naomi appeared, pale and shaken. "Let's go to my room," she said in a quiet, new voice.

"We really *do* have to zip up the scene a little," I said, opening her door. "The show may never get off the air."

"What would happen?" she asked suddenly.

"They'd cut us off. Go on with the next show," I said.

Her face deadened for a moment. She looked down, then lifted her head, taking a deep breath.

We began running the scene together quietly, our faces framed in the mirror above her dressing table. I was deliberately forcing a quicker pace to the reading of the scene by biting off cues—coming in hard on the ends of her lines. For three or four pages she kept up with me. Then suddenly there was a pause. I looked up. Naomi had closed her eyes and fainted gently, head down, onto the table.

There were seven minutes to air.

I went to the door, removed the key from the outside, pushed the lock button, and closed it quietly. There was a handkerchief sticking up out of Naomi's open purse. I held it under the water tap, wrung it out, and began daubing her forehead with it. Her head hung limply on my arm.

Someone was trying the door. There was a knock—a voice—Kate.

"We're running lines!" I yelled, picking Naomi up out of the chair and beginning to walk around the room now, jouncing her to get her going. I started the scene again in a loud voice.

"WELL, MOM! THIS IS MIDDLETOWN. ABOUT WHAT YOU EXPECTED, IS IT? GOOD TO HAVE YOU HERE, MOM!"

Naomi came to. Looking up at me in total surprise, she answered my cue as if nothing had happened. We lurched around the room, yelling the scene at each other like a couple of angry drunks.

"OK, let's go up," I said, opening the door. Kate, Hal and Gustav stood there by the doorway, ashen faced. "Here we are!" I said with a gay idiotic wave of my free hand. We made our way down the hall still shouting lines.

The ON THE AIR sign flashing urgently over the door, we entered the reverential hush of the studio. Court was in his customary place in the middle of the floor.

"OK, gang, this is the air show. Just keep that ball moving around out there. And remember, if we win this one, we could go all the way . . . twenty seconds to theme."

Naomi held my hand tightly, staring into space, saying nothing. Cameramen, crew—everyone on the floor looked quickly at us, then away. Doom hung over the studio as palpable as Spanish moss. Ralph was playing the organ theme.

For the five or so minutes that we waited together for the first act to be played, Naomi stayed standing with me, hand still in mine—a scared, aging lady—thinking (what?) thoughts.

I looked over to where the prompt men were holding the boxes for the preceding scene. Naomi had refused to consider them. What would happen if she blew? Gulping deep breaths, I continued to scan the room.

There was Kate, huddled behind a flat—alternate dresses hanging from her arm, staring balefully at the pathetic figure next to me. That beige dress three inches above the knee!

Standing in the half-light by the prop table, his body coiled and crouching like a moonlit tiger, Carl was talking to himself furiously. By his side Pepe, balancing himself on one leg, a comb in one hand, brush in the other: both of them as if waiting for a cue to spin toward Naomi like crazed ballet dancers and rip away at her with brush and Kleenex—to get rid once and for all of those sausage curls! Those deep-dish apple eyes!

Cold little runnels of sweat poured down my sides. Naomi's nerves had just given way back there in the dressing room. What now? God! I thought, this can't happen! She can't go out there and do those *things*— those *sounds*—those insane pauses!

Actors in other scenes, rather than pacing solitarily and talking to themselves, seemed riveted in odd corners— thinking only of what would happen when that light went on for Act II: Gustav, Frances, Stephanie—all standing by helplessly, like passengers on a sinking ship waiting for the last, inevitable, hull-rending wave.

The one-minute commercial break. Cameras pushing out from the previous set and turning, moving toward us; the boom truck, the cable man keeping the lines straight: a precise choreography of large and cumbersome machinery.

Suddenly I realized I was still wearing my glasses and my wedding ring. I took them off, watching, as Court gently ushered Naomi to her place. (Behind the pained half-smile his thought: "Jesus, lady, I hate to throw this cue! I'm getting the hell out of here as soon as I throw this cue!")

Behind the viewfinder of his camera, Jimmy wagging his head defeatedly as he lined up his opening shot: that closeup with the curls. (During dress rehearsal he had darted out in front of the camera, running his hands over his forehead to her with a pleading little smile. She'd looked right through him.)

Naomi and I sat facing each other. Ten seconds . . . five . . . and we began. Her knuckles were white with clutching the arm of the couch. She was speaking softly, uncertainly.

"Harlan . . . I can't tell you what it means . . . to your mother . . . for us to be together . . . it's been so hard."

The pauses were coming in the same places, but she had closed them up slightly, just enough, and varied them— filling them with a new tension. I answered. Then, as if she had received a sudden clue into the rhythm of the scene, she threw herself now into the two succeeding speeches—overlapping one of my responses, forcing me to repeat it, and jumbling my cue on the other so that I had to rephrase the beginning of my speech to match the changed words. For a moment she looked puzzled, losing her concentration by thinking back over how the mistake had been made. She had lost the sequence. A pause. A vague wave of nausea rippling through my lower abdomen.

"How was the flight?" I said.

"The flight!" she said, remembering, and clapping her hands in delighted relief. "Oh, Harlan, let me tell you . . . ." And we went on.

Once she had got going again, it was clear that out of all the chaotic fakery and overstatement she had been indulging in all day a performance was growing. I watched her "editing" now, as she went along, the distracted movements, the odd reactions, the sounds. All were coming together suddenly as she found the character. But in doing so she was also improvising again, jumbling lines, so that I was continuously snatching cues out of the air as if I were bottling fireflies.

"My goodness, I don't believe we've sat and talked like this together since you were a boy . . . " (Turning toward me. And then, as if the moment had threatened to overwhelm her, toward the camera) "a small boy—always running, restless—running—like the wind . . . . " (Her voice trailing gently.) Pure artifice, but done so magically that all of a sudden the words hardly seemed to matter. Except to me.

Somewhere, hidden, cut off, transposed—were my cues! At the same time that I was being struck by the richness of the character emerging before me, I was struggling—by telepathy, osmosis, anything—to keep up with where she was, or when she had finished.

"Oh, Harlan! . . . "

Now she was really up. Total desperation expressing itself in a haunted slackening of her jaw, a panicked stare.

"Yes, Mother?" I said, taking her hand and trying to cut through her numbness with a warm, life-giving smile.

Her body relaxed under the pressure of my grip, but instead of words, there was a breathtaking display of being. Tears came. The thick mascara began to run down her cheeks. With a quick, girlish gesture she wiped the tears away, leaving a smudge, then teased two persimmon curls away from her forehead. Those crazy curls, the Mata Hari mascara, the foolishly short skirt suddenly fit this soft, vulnerable woman. Poignant. Marvelous. But where were the words? My cue!

The teleprompter man, his complexion gone a kind of mauve, was stalking Naomi now from under camera two —jabbing his finger ferociously toward the words. She disdained him, tugging instead at the too short beige dress and repeating my name with a sigh.

Finally, desperately, he turned the box around, looked at the words himself and hissed toward her, "Fader! His fader!"

The sound of the strange voice seemed to jar her out of her wonder momentarily.

"Father," she said wistfully, then subsided again.

"Do you think I look like Father?" I said. (My voice, saying the strange line, sounded to me like something being shouted up out of a well.)

"Oh, Harlan," she repeated, as if re-entering the atmosphere, "I look at you . . . (Yes? Yes!) and I see your father . . . (Beautiful!) so strongly." (That's my baby!)

She was doing an unforgettable thing now, out of that chaotic moment. She put her hands to her lips, looked down at herself briefly, and then held her hands out toward me, her head tilted like an inquisitive child's— illuminating the character, the relationship, the scene in a flash of light. This was not an actress impersonating a character, but an essence imposing itself on the environment. Naomi was creating Grace Cross out of herself—by accident, by mirrors, by being the only thing she was capable of being, a star.

She came toward me now, this oddly poignant figure. Ralph's organ notes building dimly. Grace and Harlan embracing tenderly. The scene faded and was over.

Court, beaming relievedly, pressed his finger to his

nose indicating that we had not only got through, but had picked up our two and a half minutes as well.

The other actors, having gathered around the two monitors at either end of the studio, came toward us in a rush —tense, excited. It was beautiful, they said.

Gustav was at my side, holding my arm in a vise-like grip.

"My God, old cock, I don't know how you did all that. You were fantastic! But you know, it looked marvelous. Come on, let's run *our* scene now."

Another scene! In the haze of the moment, I'd forgotten there was another scene. Every line of it seemed to have flown out of my head. Gustav and I walked to the other end of the studio whispering the scene back and forth and standing in place for our cue.

Naomi waited on the floor for me to finish, and then we walked quietly out of the studio, during the final commercial break, to her dressing room. Inside we looked at each other and laughed suddenly.

"Christ!" she exclaimed, flopping down into her chair. "How do you do this every day?"

"It's not quite like this every day," I said.

"I know I gave you some funny cues out there."

"That's all right," I said. "We did it. It's done."

"Think we did OK?" she asked.

"You were great," I said.

The wet, rolled-up handkerchief still lay on the dressing table. She picked it up idly, stared at it for a moment, then looked up at me.

"Thanks," she said.

"Got your locker key?" I asked. "Nothing means anything if you've lost that locker key."

She fished the key out of her pocketbook. "Got it," she said, brushing a few raspberry curls back from her brow.

There was a knock at the door. I opened it to Hal and Max. Hal had a rose in his hand, still dripping from having been snatched out of the bunch of flowers on Terry's desk.

"The switchboard is jammed with calls!" he said, presenting Naomi with the rose.

"The client just called from Chicago," added Max. "He said the scene was very moving. And it *was*—touching. Everyone is excited."

I moved out of the room. Max came out into the hall after me.

"Steven."

I turned around.

"Thanks," said Max.

"Never mind that. Where's my balloon?" I said.

As I passed the office on the way to my room, Terry was on the phone. Two other phones were ringing furiously. Terry waved distractedly for help and I sat down and began answering calls with her. In a steady flow— people were calling to say how wonderful the show had been; how much it had meant to them; how touching Naomi was and how much they were coming to love Harlan. How happy they were. How moved.

Hal came in then to take over the other phones.

"They seemed to love the show," I said, smiling.

I dressed quickly and walked out into the balmy late afternoon. Bound for home, I began to think of all those people calling like that. And of how, for every one of them, for every voice, every affectionate word, there were hundreds of thousands like them—having the same thoughts, feeling the same love at that very moment in time—on that warm summer afternoon. Awesome.

SEVEN

In the excitement over Naomi Talbot's triumph in the face of seeming disaster—coming, as it did, on the heels of Jennifer Dryden's fleshy assaults on my equilibrium—I hadn't quite kept track of what was happening. But finally, given some brooding time, I began now to see the larger picture. We were entering a new transitional phase in the saga of Harlan Cross. From rapacious eagle, soaring over Middletown snatching virgins out of cribs, I was obviously entering solidly now into my kiwi bird period. From doer to done upon.

I was a good guy now, caught in a rivalry between mother and girlfriend: a conflict guaranteed to warm the cockles of twelve million hearts. I would come home from the hospital in the evening, and there would be Mom, sitting, knitting scarves and doilies. There would be layer cakes baking in the oven with favorite fillings from Harlan's childhood.

"Remember how you loved chocolate?"

And bango! Out would come a faded snapshot of me in a sailor suit eating a piece of chocolate cake.

"Remember that? Your daddy took that. Remember that sailor suit? I made that for you."

Closeup of Harlan remembering. "Yes, Mother, I remember."

"And here you are wearing your daddy's army hat and pretending to smoke his pipe. Remember that? Such a little man!"

"Still got that pipe, Mother?"

"All your father's pipes. Stored away. Memories . . . memories."

"And the hat?"

"Oh, yes."

Grace, pushing her persimmon curls back over her forehead wistfully, and flicking out snapshots like a canasta dealer.

"The lodge in Lake Placid. There we are swimming."

"Swimming. Yes."

"There's Daddy on a horse. How he loved to ride! Remember?"

"I remember that."

In the first two weeks, there were three snapshot scenes, two scenes of eating Mother's completely home-cooked meals—especially layer cakes—and three trips to the park by the church, which quickly became Grace Cross's favorite spot in Middletown.

"I love this little park, Harlan."

"It's pretty, isn't it?"

"Oh, indeed. It reminds me so much of Augusta."

"Augusta?"

"Remember when Daddy was stationed in Georgia during the war and we had that lovely little cottage in Augusta?"

"Oh, right, yes."

"Surely you haven't forgotten."

"No, no—the little cottage, of course."

"And there was that little church . . . was it Methodist or Episcopalian? I've forgotten. Anyway the church with that little park nearby. I remember how you used to love to run and play. There was a little playground with swings and teeter totters. And I was always after you about scuffing your shoes."

Sudden closeup of Harlan, remembering.

"Do you know, Harlan, I've still got those shoes somewhere. Bronzed."

The set for the little park was Naomi's favorite. Sitting there, batting her great eyes, fondling twigs and smelling flowers, she would launch into nostalgia-dipped reminiscences about Augusta and playgrounds and scuffed shoes with heart-rending gusto. A star reborn. Interrupted by occasional intercuts of the back of my head, she played to the camera as if it were an old beau: smiling, nodding, and making sounds. Naomi felt more comfortable with monologues. She could jumble the words around and talk about shoes before swimming, or pipes instead of horses, and it wouldn't make much difference. I would grunt along with whatever she said and we could generally keep going.

"Oh, by the way, Harlan. I guess it just slipped my mind. Your friend Miss Williams called last night, while you were out on call."

"Susan?"

"Yes. I think that was her name."

(A constrained note coming into Naomi's voice. An arching of brows, tense smile.)

"She asked if we might like to come for dinner one night next week."

"Well, would you, Mother?"

"If you'd like to, certainly."

(Dropped lids. The mouth set in magnanimous acceptance.)

"Sure. You'll like her. She's a lovely girl."

(A pause for self-gathering.)

"I'm sure I will. Oh, my—just look at those tulips! Remember those beautiful tulips in Augusta, Harlan?"

"Tulips?"

When not playing kiwi to Naomi's bird of paradise I could be seen trotting around after Dr. Susan Williams, who in her Peter Pan way was becoming responsive enough not to blanch when I squeezed her hand under the cafeteria table or stole a kiss in the lab office.

But, of course, there was her palsied aunt to think about. And the free clinics. And Harlan's mother, filling his apartment with layer cakes and snapshots and tulips.

As moments alone became more difficult to come by, and the dual role of patient swain and loyal son more and more demanding, the stage directions describing Harlan's appearance became progressively trodden:

"*Sad*," "*Rueful*," "*Torn*," "*Dejected*," "*Anxious*."

As for the dialogue, I was given to express myself more and more in exhausted monosyllables and confused chirps. What to do with my voice became a problem. And my face. The vocal attack I had used for the old Harlan seemed out of place now. I began changing it. And my expression—once constantly alert, sharp, grinning, confident—began collapsing into a kind of passive imbecility.

"You always look so worried, Steven."

My mother, my *real* one, was calling with her monthly report.

"Well, they've got me doing a lot of worrying," I said, cleverly.

"And your eyes look so . . . haunted."

"Haunted?"

"Haggard."

"Haggard too? That's really terrific."

"Oh, I'm sorry, I didn't mean . . . you know . . . ."

"Still got a lot of hair on the back of my head though," I said.

"But," my mother continued, "I do think it's so exciting that you're playing with Naomi Talbot! Such a great lady. Mrs. Jessup is just thrilled."

"I thought she would be," I said.

"What's going to happen with Susan? Are you getting engaged?"

"It looks that way."

"Mrs. Jessup thinks that you're going to get Susan pregnant and Grace Cross is going to try to kill herself."

"Kill herself?"

"But I told her that you wouldn't get Susan in trouble. Not the way you are now—so considerate and everything.

133

I told her that in time Grace will just have to accept losing you again. I mean, that's life, isn't it?"

"Yes, that's . . . . "

"Susan is such a nice girl—quiet and sweet. I like her. Everyone does. I've gotten so many calls. We're all so relieved. I mean after that awful Lisa. And that silly business with Nancy! Paul and Nancy are happy again, aren't they?"

"Very happy."

"By the way, Steven, Mrs. Jessup asked me about your voice."

"My voice?"

"She thinks it sounds a bit faint."

"A bit faint, huh?"

"I told her it was probably your hay fever coming on again."

"Hay fever? I never had hay fever."

"Yes you did."

"No, never."

"I remember distinctly," insisted my mother, "you said you had hay fever."

"Wait a minute!" I said. "That's Harlan."

"What?"

"Harlan had the hay fever. Not me."

"I told Mrs. Jessup that's probably what it was. Don't you remember, you mentioned it to Ruth Markham."

"Frances?"

"No, Ruth."

"I . . . . "

"That you'd had hay fever as a boy."

"OK," I repeated numbly, "I had hay fever as a boy. I guess I forgot that. Well, it's been nice talking to you, Mother."

For a strange moment I thought I'd been talking to Grace Cross. Who was that staring at me in the hallway mirror? Steven? Harlan? Was I on? Did somebody call places? And what *were* those worry lines? Those funny new creases? Were they Harlan's? Mine?

"Who was that on the phone?" asked Angela.

"My mother. She says I have hay fever."

"Hay fever?"

"She says I looked haunted."

We stared at the mirror together.

"Of course," said Angela after a moment, "I see you every day."

"So does she."

"But she's seeing you as Harlan."

"Well, that's . . . yes," I said.

Angela put her arm in mine, and we struck a pose, as if for an old-fashioned wedding picture.

"Remember the old Harlan?" I said.

"Show me," said Angela.

I made a face in the mirror like the old Harlan—the arrogance, the knife-like grin.

"Oh, look!" said Angela.

"Terrific?"

"Yes," said Angela soulfully.

"Good old Harlan," I said, holding the expression and leaning into the mirror. The lines were gone.

Watching the old Harlan slip away from me like a loved one in a bad dream wasn't to be my only new and favorite spectator sport. There was an emotional tennis match brewing between Naomi and Jennifer Dryden that was threatening to keep me moving around too.

Generally speaking, the foxhole camaraderie between performers on daytime serials survives various-sized differences. And as for outward hostility, there just isn't time. But the relationship between Naomi and Jennifer seemed to disintegrate before it began and to proceed downhill immediately afterwards.

Jennifer's style: her cool, her youth, her easy sensuality, irritated Naomi to distraction. And as far as Jennifer was concerned, all that "star stuff" of Naomi's, the "grand old lady" bit, was "like nowhere."

During a break between Acts I and V of a morning rehearsal Jennifer popped into my room as I was attempting a nap on my boy scout surplus cot. She asked if I was asleep, and then found enough space to accommodate herself sideways on the cot, facing me—her hands, buried in a profusion of blond silk hair, supporting a quizzically tilted head.

"I mean I don't want to bug you or anything." She stared past my eyes at the wall, musing.

"What's the matter?" I said.

"How can you stand that old dame?" said Jennifer.

"You mean Naomi?"

"Yeah. The way you have to carry her in every scene, and like everybody's supposed to fuss over her and kow-tow. All that star stuff—that really bugs me."

"She *is* a star," I said. "She's earned a certain amount of kow-tow."

Jennifer was silent for a moment.

"I don't go for all that. I mean like she's a member of the company now, like you or anybody, and they're paying her, right? I mean, she ought to know the words, for one thing. Don't you think?"

"Yeah," I said. "Except she's not used to this. It's very different for her."

"Well, I could never screw up and flop around like that and like feel right, could you?"

"No, I don't believe I could," I said.

"If I was a star," continued Jennifer, "I mean—I'd work real hard, and be like nice to everybody—make them feel, I don't know, good."

"You'd make a nice star," I said.

"Yeah," said Jennifer pensively. She looked at me for a moment, thinking. "You know," she continued, "you really *are* a prince—a real one, I mean like a real hero—always saving that old chick in every scene."

"You're just saying that because I'm always walking around with my hands behind my back and waving to people from coaches," I said.

"You'd be a groovy prince," said Jennifer, laughing.

"I'll tell you what," I said. "When I'm a real prince and you're a real star, you can ride around in my coach with me and wave to people."

Jennifer waved her hand.

"No," I said. "Like this." With hand held straight out, I made the small, circular gesture of a princely wave.

"Hey, that's neat," she said, imitating me. A girl in an angora sweater dress, smiling and waving at imaginary crowds, like any good believer.

Official hostilities between Naomi and Jennifer did not begin, however, until the morning of the first big "triangle" scene: Grace, Susan, and Harlan having dinner at Susan's apartment.

When I arrived at the rehearsal hall, Naomi was sitting at the long table scowling at her script, and Jennifer stood—spread legged, one hand on a far-flung hip, idly doodling on the blackboard at the far end of the room. She wore a flesh-colored micro mini about the size of an ace bandage and a matching skin-tight jersey.

"Good morning, ladies," I said.

"Hi," said Jennifer, brushing chalk from her hands and idling toward me for a good morning kiss.

Behind us there was the rattle of Naomi's script.

"Good morning, Steven," came the voice like a harbor noise. "If you're getting coffee, I'd like another cup myself." If the rest of us accepted Jennifer as a scenic wonder that deserves to be allowed certain extravagances, Naomi was not about to be that generous. As Jennifer floated into closeup, Naomi stared critically and bared her teeth.

I mover toward the coffee machine. "How about you, Jennifer?" I said.

"No thanks," said Jennifer, sitting opposite Naomi at the table, then tipping the chair backwards with an arch of her back and crossing her long legs.

"Jennifer doesn't drink coffee, apparently," said Naomi, taking the cup from me without shifting her gaze. "Why not, dear? Is it flattening or something?"

Jennifer smiled slowly—the two looking at each other steadily. I wondered what had been said before I got there. If anything.

"How long have you two been here?"

"Little while," said Jennifer, her legs straddling the chair now and rocking it back and forth. "Just sort of like standing around."

"Or sitting," added Naomi.

Max came rushing in. "Sorry I'm late, people. Couldn't get the damn car going."

The scene was a long one, taking up the first two acts. It began with Susan greeting Grace and Harlan at the door of her apartment. Then the introductions, the serving of drinks, polite chatter, and the announcement by Susan at the end of Act I that dinner was ready. Act II was dinner.

Actors approach the first blocking rehearsal in various ways. Some have memorized the lines cold and don't like the idea of having to refer to a script at all in the morning. They try as well as possible to remember the moves as the director gives them. Others carry their scripts to jot down the blocking, rather than try to deal with words and moves right off the bat. Just about everybody, however, goes without the script for the second running of the scene. After that there are only three more run-throughs before the air show, and most of us—especially the director—want the security of getting the scenes "on their feet" and running at the approximate pace they will finally be played at. This done there is less likelihood of line, time, and playing problems during camera run-throughs in the studio.

Naomi, however, seemed to consider the air show as if it were some distant mirage toward which she could stumble fitfully like a lost desert soldier. In her mind she was still making pictures—spending a day on a two-page scene, thirty or forty takes, a thousand feet of film from which the two or three minutes could be perfectly edited. However much Hal and Max tried to make her see that this was a totally different kind of ball game we were playing she seemed to drift back to the idea that she was making a movie, or doing a play with four weeks of rehearsal to loll around in.

Mumbling her lines in her usual rehearsal voice, making notes in her script, at times burying her face in it and ignoring the actors around her, she stalked and walked around the scenes like someone having an angry dream. Then she would stop dead in her tracks to pepper Max with questions:

"Why is she sitting while I'm standing?"

"Why don't I get the drink now?"

"Why do I move to the window here?"

"Does she have to stand next to me like that?"

She and Jennifer were the focus of the scenes: the jealous rivals—Susan defensively accommodating, Grace aggressively polite. I was doing Harlan's "gray eminence" bit, looking from one to the other with conciliatory smiles, and chirping monosyllables like a referee in a ping pong tournament.

Jennifer's voice, cool and slangy, began to join Max's now in Naomi's question and answer game.

"It will be closeups there, and I need you standing."

"So I'm like tall, like so what?"

"Going to the window gives Susan time to go to the kitchen and come back with the drinks."

"Anyway, it's not very groovy to lean way over to pour . . . ."

"We've only got ten minutes, ladies."

"Was that my cue? Like I can't hear you, Naomi."

War was being declared. And I was the Red Cross observer, making sure the wounded would be cared for, the prisoners properly treated.

Actors waiting to run succeeding scenes sat with their coffee and pastry and newspapers, watching raptly as the tension grew.

Terry, trying to get a timing on the second act, sat clicking her stopwatch off and on as if she had found a wonderful new exercise for the thumb. The scene, an intricate one full of eating and serving and plate shuffling (all done in dumb show, without props) kept coughing to a halt like a failing jalopy.

At one point, Jennifer, niftily pantomiming serving an imaginary slice of London broil, knocked Naomi's script off the table.

"What is it?" snapped Naomi.

"London broil," I said. "If yours is too rare, I'll send it back."

"I mean what's the line?"

Terry cued her, "I'd love a bit more, thank you."

"That's what I thought," pounced Naomi. "How can I ask for more after she's just served me! That *is* what you were doing, wasn't it?" she said, turning on Jennifer truculently.

"Yeah," said Jennifer, easing out of her prim Susan Williams pose and thrusting a hip. "Only so what? I mean you could just say 'Thank you.' What's so groovy about 'Love a bit more'? I mean it's not exactly Shakespeare or anything, or like the big moment in the scene, you know?" She slid one leg indolently over the other and looked up at the clock.

"It's a line in the scene!" said Naomi, gathering herself up in the chair and swiveling her head like an aroused condor. "One of *my* lines in the scene!"

"So you forgot it—big deal!" said Jennifer. "I'm sorry I knocked your line on the floor."

"It's really wonderful sitting here watching two real pros work," I said toward the pastry and coffee cups. Max was standing, his hands held in the air like a holdup victim. "Would you like a little London broil while you're waiting?" I said.

Remembering what Jennifer had said to me about Naomi that other morning in my dressing room, I could see that she was making it a point of honor not to give way to the older woman on anything and to let her know that as far as Jennifer was concerned, Naomi's behavior was simply fake.

"Like I'm *all kinds* of sorry!" repeated Jennifer, gaining volume.

"Ladies, ladies," said Max, his held-up hands waving pencils.

Naomi decided to make some real noise.

"Goddam it, I can't work under these conditions! There's no time to *do* anything! Nothing works. No props! No furniture! No time!"

Hal rushed over, a death smile painted on his face—to placate, to solve.

"Kiddo, sweetheart!" he said.

"Huh?" said Naomi, spinning on him.

"Honey, Nami, baby!" Hal continued, going at her like

a Japanese wrestler, and managing a hand around her shoulder.

The phone rang. It was the writers. The script was three and a half minutes short, and they were phoning in additional dialogue. Terry was on with them, taking down the words in shorthand. Three and a half minutes of dialogue about London broil and asparagus and unseasonal weather being phoned in all the way from Stonehenge.

Naomi was being walked back and forth now like a post-operative patient finally making it around the sun deck.

"Goddam it!" she continued. "There's enough pressure around here without comments from some ingenue with a staple in her navel!"

"You and me, baby!" said Hal, grinning, patting, walking.

Jennifer was back at the blackboard, drawing things.

Gustav had spilled his coffee all over the floor plan.

Terry was reading the new dialogue to Max and answering the phone again.

Bill Seivers, back from vacation and sporting a tan, sat reading a treatise on witchcraft—serene, oblivious, practicing flight in his astral body. I borrowed a dime from him and went out into the hall to call home. Suddenly I wanted to hear Angela's voice—warm and sleepy—and ask her about the fish and how the weather looked outside.

"What's happened?" said Angela. "Are you all right?"

"Yeah, I'm OK. There's a lot of yelling going on around here."

"Yelling?"

"Yeah. How're the fish?"

"The fish? Fine. I just fed them."

"Good. And Chipper?"

"He's sleeping in his box."

"Chris get off to school OK?"

"Sure."

"Good. OK."

"Are you sure you're all right?"

"Yeah, I'm terrific. I'll see you later. Goodby."

"Goodby, darling."

When I came back to the room Naomi's voice was still rising. Hal was still walking her. Suddenly I felt like yelling too.

"All right, goddam it! This is your captain speaking! Now I just want to tell you that my partner and I will not fly this crate another five hundred feet with all this noise going on! Right, Gus?"

"Noisy shvine!" screamed Gustav, quickly becoming my co-pilot.

"Now my co-captain here, Captain Reiner, drank a lot of near beer last night in Milwaukee, and although he speaks very little English he's said enough to convince me that if there's any more yelping out of you he's going to come back there with a ray gun and let you all have it. Right, Gus?"

"Shvine!" repeated Gustav.

"As I say, Captain Reiner isn't too fluid in the language, but he sure as hell knows how to fire a ray gun—I can assure you of that!"

"This place is a madhouse!" yelled Max.

Naomi had quieted down and was gathering her things. Hal got into it. "This is Hal baby, calling from control tower 31."

"Go ahead, Hal baby, we read you. This is Captain Prince, or Prince Captain, depending on what meter you're reading."

"Dear Prince Captain—I love you," said Hal.

"Shvine!" screamed Gustav.

Max was standing on a chair now, stamping and waving his pencil. "Does the fact that we have a show to put on in six hours get to anybody here?"

"Who's that noisy passenger in the space shoes?" said Hal.

Gustav and I ran at Max, pinning him at either side and rushing him out of the rehearsal hall, around in a few circles and back again without breaking stride.

"Madhouse!" yelled Max.

Stunned into silence, Naomi Talbot walked past us out of the room.

Although tension had been eased for the moment, it became clear within the hour that this was going to be a more than usually difficult day. A seam had sprung open somewhere, forces unleashed, a full-moon madness filled the air.

Chiefly there was the business of Naomi and Jennifer. It became difficult to tell now, as we ran the scenes, where the antagonism between the characters they were playing left off and where it began between the two women themselves. Hiding her essential self behind the Peter Pan front of Susan Williams day after day had begun to have its effect on Jennifer. A born-free look coming into the prim Susan Williams gaze—animal energy getting ready to unleash itself against the blurred Naomi-Grace image that loomed up suddenly—imperious, taunting. And Naomi, all unretracted claws and hostile sausage curls, staring balefully across the space between her and the hated rival: Jennifer-Susan, that nubile bunny rabbit, breathing chestily behind the fake high-necked Simplicity pattern goody gumdrop virginity blouse. That mercilessly young, menacingly cool son-grabber:

Grace

Well, Miss Williams, we meet at last. Harlan has told me so much about you.

Susan

(*Smiling pleasantly*) Good things, I hope.

Grace

Indeed yes. (*Looking over the room*) What a sweet little apartment.

Susan

Thank you.

Grace

Do you plan to stay here long?

Susan

Why, yes. Pinewood is a fine hospital. I'm very happy there.

Grace

Well then, I imagine you'll be thinking of buying your own furniture by and by.

Susan

(*Uneasily*) But this *is* my own furniture, Mrs. Cross.

Grace

Oh, my! I'm so sorry. I thought you were new.

Susan

Well, I . . . .

Grace

I got the impression from Harlan that you had only recently met.

Harlan

We had known each other before.

Susan

(*Trying bravely to rise to the occasion*) We didn't see each other very much when Harlan first came to Pinewood. He's a surgeon and I'm an internist . . . and anyway, he always seemed so busy . . . and . . . .

Grace

I see. Well, Harlan has always been industrious and popular. I remember when he was a boy . . . .

Harlan

(*Discomfited*) Mother, we don't want to hear about how wonderful I was as a boy.

Max's voice interrupted over the P.A. "Naomi, could you sit lower in your chair? I'm shooting over your downstage shoulder here, and you're blocking Jennifer out of the shot."

"You want me to slouch?" said Naomi. "I don't think Grace would slouch."

"All right, we'll switch chairs." Two grips quickly appeared out of the shadows to rearrange the chairs.

"By the way," said Jennifer, staring at Naomi coolly, "you like cut me twice in there."

"What?" said Naomi, spinning around.

"Yeah. Twice. Where I say 'Well not really I' and when

I say 'he always seemed so busy, and seemed to have so many friends.' "

"What exactly did I cut?" demanded Naomi, walking toward Jennifer purposefully.

"You cut 'Not really I,' and 'seemed to have so many friends,' " said Jennifer levelly.

"I'm simply trying to get *pace* into the scene!" Naomi snapped.

The grips trundled off the set and Court was speaking up into the boom mike.

"Chairs are ready, Max."

"If you wouldn't hem and haw so oddly, I'd know where the cutoffs were," continued Naomi.

"The cutoffs come when I've like said all my words," said Jennifer, getting up out of the chair. "And I'm like 'hemming' and 'hawing' because I'm supposed to be bugged."

"Bugged?"

"Uncertain. OK?"

Max's voice cut through again. "What's happening? What are we waiting for?"

Naomi wasn't finished. "Maybe you'd like to give me a little signal when you're through with each speech."

Court was touching Naomi's arm. "We're ready, ladies."

"Let's go, please," said Max.

"Where from?" I yelled.

"From Harlan's line 'we don't want to hear how wonderful I was as a boy.' "

Naomi, halfway back to her new chair, had another thought. "Or you could hold up a little sign that said 'I am finished' on it."

"For Christ's sake," I said, "let's go—I'm getting a tan out here!"

Harlan

Mother, we don't want to hear about how wonderful I was as a boy.

Grace

Who doesn't?

                              Susan
(*Trying to be pleasant*) I'd love to hear about it.
                              Grace
Thank you. You know . . . .

Naomi was dry suddenly. "What's the line?" she said impatiently. "I'm so busy keeping my shoulder down so I won't *block* people, and my voice slow so I won't *cut* them! What is it?"

Court gave her the line. She started again:

                              Grace
Thank you, dear. You know when Harlan was nine years old, he had the most . . . .

"What is it?"

"Prosperous," said Court.

"Prosperous what?" said Naomi, rattled. She was getting into some of the new material that had been added that morning.

"Oh, Christ! This is that new stuff!"

"That's right," said Max over the P.A.

"Haven't we got enough to worry about without new material?"

"Sorry, dear, it's a matter of time," said Max.

"Time, time, time!"

"That's three times," I said loudly. "One more, and the other team can just run out the clock."

"What?" said Naomi.

We struggled on, stopping and starting for boom shadows, mike problems, line dries. There was no food to work with. Wouldn't be any, of course, until dress rehearsal. Naomi fumed. Jennifer, on the other hand, was cooling it: getting all her words, always staying within her character, winning her war with Naomi Talbot by sheer professional grit. The girl had character.

In fact, sympathy for Naomi was preceptibly lessening

in all quarters. Her demands, her petulant outbursts, were being met with blank looks now.

Even Hal looked grim when we broke for lunch. As I walked out of the studio to go to my dressing room he and Max were huddled with Naomi outside the control room, speaking in urgent-looking sotto voce.

Halfway through my hamburger there was a knock at the door. It was Naomi, dudgeon rising, looking for agreement from somebody about how impossible everything was. How nothing worked properly. How Jennifer was annoying the hell out of her. And *now*, how Hal and Max were adding insult to injury by asking *her* to be more cooperative! She was striding around the room, her voice bouncing ship-whistle noises off the walls, hands flying, arms flailing.

"Look!" I said, suddenly jumping up out of my chair. "You're marvelous in the part and everybody respects that. But you're getting a lot of help, which you don't seem to realize, and you're making a lot of noise, and wasting a lot of time! We survive by *time* here. This *ain't* the movies! Or Broadway! And you just ruined my hamburger!"

Naomi went rigid. "Are you finished?" she said. The words came out as if she were speaking through a wired jaw.

"Not yet," I said. "I'm going to start fining you a quarter for every wrong cue you throw me, and at the rate you're going, I'll be able to buy myself a small island in the Pacific by the end of the year!"

"That's a rotten thing to say!" she yelled, moving to the door. But I jumped in front of her.

"I sit there under those lights like a beached whale while you run around kvetching about everything!"

"How dare you!" sputtered Naomi, looking around for something heavy.

"Because I'm your son!" I advanced on her, glinting maniacally. "And because I'm a prince! You didn't know that, did you?" I added, continuing to move in on her, my hands behind my back; then circling her in a slouching shuffle and flicking ashes from an imaginary cigar.

"Oh, Emily, can't you see, I love you!" I said, grabbing her around the waist and forcing her into a tango. "Won't you say you'll learn your lines for me? Oh, Emily, I can just see us in our little home—rehearsing. I can see you there—leaning over a hot stove. Only I can't see the stove!"

"You crazy bastard!" yelled Naomi, pushing out of my grasp.

"Oh, Emily! Learn your lines!" I shouted again. But she was gone.

During the after-lunch run-through, Naomi kept shooting sidelong glances at me and being terribly quiet. I also noticed that during the dress rehearsal she used the teleprompter to get herself out of a brief "dry." The scenes were smoothing out, going well.

During notes after dress, Max asked about a particular bit during the eating scene in Act V.

"Oh, yes," said Naomi grimly, "that was my fault. I passed the plate late and made Jennifer delay the line." There was a pause. Everyone tried not to look amazed. Naomi looked around quickly.

"OK," said Max, checking off the note on his clipboard. "As far as the acting goes, it's a perf." He turned to confer with Andy about a lighting change.

"What's a 'perf'?" asked Naomi, leaning over to me and whispering. It was the first time she'd spoken to me since our antic chat in my dressing room.

" 'Perf' for 'perfect,' " I whispered back to her. "When you don't get an acting note—that's a perf."

"You mean he thought we were perf?"

"Yeah, but what does *he* know?" I said.

"Let's run through the scene," she said. "Where's Jennifer?" It was the first time Naomi had ever suggested running a scene after dress rehearsal. She usually spent the time running around about her hair, or seeing Kate about her costume, or fussing over makeup.

Jennifer, controlling her surprise, joined us and we went into the studio together.

"Let's just walk it around," I said. (Prowling around

before the air show is a religion with me. Sitting still before having to act would be like coming off the bench to pinch hit.)

Like three strollers on a boardwalk, we paced the length and breadth of the studio, chatting the lines quietly to each other. We passed Gustav practicing his Act III monologue with appropriate gestures in transit several times—he ignored us totally.

Frances stood in a corner, as she always does, her script spread neatly before her on the prop table, mumbling politely to herself. Stephanie and Alan were working out a blocking change in their living room. Court, wearing his headset, his ubiquitous plastic cigarette drooping from his lips, sat napping in an overstuffed chair.

"Let's do Act IV one more time," said Naomi, walking between us, stopping to mime a bit of business from time to time.

The day that had begun badly ended well, with everything coming together in the final hours the way you always hope it will.

"We were perf!" said Naomi afterwards, elated by the good work we'd done since the chaotic morning. She looked at Jennifer. "Forget this morning, all right? Steven said I was doing quite a lot of 'kvetching,' whatever that is, and he's such a smart-ass that I suppose he's never wrong." She made a face at me and walked off. Jennifer looked after her with amazement, then toward me.

"Either the days are getting longer around here, or my watch has stopped," I said, as we started for the stairs toward our rooms.

EIGHT

If the writers of daytime serials can ever be said to have fun they certainly have fun with time—moulding and stretching it and playing with it as if it were so much silly putty. A half-hour show can represent a week or ten minutes, depending on the writers' needs. Winter can be dispensed with in four days, or seven weeks can take eleven months. Weekends, of course, are out. They are referred to but never lived. It is a life made up of Mondays to Fridays, during which time can stop anywhere along the line. For example if on Wednesday one of the story lines involves a courtroom trial, and another a serious operation and recovery, it might be a week or two before you get to Thursday.

Somehow, however, the mystical calendars of daytime serials seem to have a final and acceptable logic. Life seems to keep happening even when it stands as still as statuary.

For Harlan Cross, life was taking forever. Time had stopped as dead as if Harlan and Grace and Susan were three Stonehenge boulders measuring history by dawns and sunsets. There were still layer cakes and tulips, of course, and snapshots, and visits to the little park by the church. Still operations to perform, and records to be listened to in Susan's apartment. There were hand holdings, and wistful chats insinuating that something would *happen* eventually. We would be engaged. Yes! That was it! Someday. And someday after that—married!

But things were always happening to stall events. The palsied aunt put us off several weeks of story time which stretched out to two months of actual time. Grace got sick. That took a month. Obviously, the Harlan-Grace-Susan triangle was considered to have enough suspended staying power to keep us circling each other for—how long? Indefinitely? forever?

Visions suggested themselves of Susan losing her youth waiting for an aging and paunched Harlan to say the final words. While Grace, ancient and toothless, gumming her way through an infinity of layer cakes, still stood jealous vigil over their ruined lives.

My fan mail took a new and definite turn. All the old hatred was long since gone, replaced by love and concern. Letters ending with a profusion of warmest regards, best wishes, and bless you's.

Ladies in Gristede's grew maternal when they recognized me now, rooting among the avocadoes and pears and peaches.

"This one looks nice and ripe, doctor."

"Thanks so much."

Mike, my bartender friend at Foley's, was full of smiles and approval at the turn events had taken.

"My God, Steven, I can't tell you what it's meant to my mother!"

"Pleased, is she?"

"Pleased! Why, she's that thrilled and happy! You've become her favorite, and that's no lie."

"That's very nice," I said.

"And you remember she'd about given up on you, you know—with all them rotten things you was doin' before."

"Yes," I said. "She threw her hip out of joint again, didn't she?"

"Beside herself she was! But then when it come out that Harlan had a mother . . . . "

"Changed the whole picture for her, huh?" I said.

"That's it exactly. Changed the picture, yes," said Mike.

"And Harlan's patience and loyalty, you know—not wanting to let his mother go back on her own until she's settled in her mind, you know."

"It's taking her a long time to settle her mind though," I said.

"Well now listen, Steven." Mike leaned across the bar, his awesome forearms matching strangely the high, hushed cathedral tone of his voice. "It's hard for a woman alone, you know." He cocked his head slightly, leaving me a cauliflowered ear to whisper back into. (Better not kid around. Those forearms.)

"Absolutely. You're right," I said.

He turned his face back to mine. "A man can have many friends and many women in his life," he said, his voice quivering slightly now, "but a man only has one mother." He gave me the ear again.

"Absolutely true!" I shouted quickly.

"Well," said Mike, straightening up, "are you going to marry the pretty young doctor, or what?"

"I'm trying," I said chirpily.

"Been quite some time, hasn't it?" said Mike.

"Yes," I gloomed.

"Well, you know, the old lady *could* move in with you for the time being."

"Until she was settled in her mind?"

"Exactly, yes," said Mike. "You know, that Grace Cross was a real looker in her time. I seen a lot of her pictures. Some lovely piece she was. Listen, do you think you could get her to sign a photo for my mother? She asked me to ask you."

"You mean Naomi Talbot? Sure," I said.

"That'll be very nice. Say, how long have you been on the show now?"

"How long?" I said. I was "up." Completely blank. How long?

"Well, let's see," I said. "Next month I'll be eighty-two . . . ."

Customers at the other end of the bar were calling for service. Mike turned toward them.

"I gotta go," I said.

"Go and pop the question to the pretty doctor, why don't cha," said Mike over his shoulder as he moved down the bar.

I paid the bill and walked out into the crowded street. How long? Why didn't I know? I used to know right away. God, I was losing track! No events to measure time by any more. When wasn't I on the show? People, scenes, characters began rolling through my mind—Lisa, Rick Mallory. Events, changes. Then the stopping of time. Naomi and Jennifer and I playing the same scenes over and over again like amnesia victims:

Act IV

Fade In:
Susan's apartment. Night.
Harlan and Susan have just returned from dinner. He is putting on a record (something quiet and classical). He moves over to the couch next to Susan. She has a faraway look.

Harlan

What are you thinking?

Susan

Oh, nothing.

Harlan

Come on, I know that look.

Susan

All right. I was thinking about us. About how nice it would be if we could just get married and settle down together. And there didn't have to be all this . . . this waiting and uncertainty.

Harlan

I know. It's too bad life has to be so complicated.

Susan

Does it, Harlan? Does it have to be so complicated?

Harlan

If my mother hadn't become ill . . . .

Susan

(*Resignedly*) I know.

Harlan

We've discussed her living with us.

Susan

Yes.

Harlan

You said yourself it would never work out. It wouldn't be fair to you. And just letting her go off alone now wouldn't be fair to her.

Susan

I guess life just isn't very fair sometimes. I just wish we had more time together. It would make the waiting easier.

Harlan

I know. Between my mother and your aunt and our work . . . .

Susan

Yes.

(*The music continues to play, Brahms perhaps. Harlan and Susan sit quietly now—half listening, half engrossed in their own thoughts.*)

Remember the old Harlan? Life was never too complicated for *him!* Remember the old fire? The old chutzpah? The ruthlessness?

Act V

Fade In:
Harlan's apartment. Later that night. Harlan is opening the front door. He turns on the light in the living room. We hear Grace's voice calling out from her bedroom.

Grace

Harlan? Is that you?

154

Harlan

(*Throwing his jacket wearily on the couch*) Yes, mother. You still awake? (*He moves toward her door. Opens it. Grace is sitting up in bed eating a piece of cake.*)

Grace

I couldn't sleep. It's so late. Look at the time.

Harlan

Well, I'm afraid I lost track of it.. There was no reason for you to stay up, though.

Grace

I worry about you, dear. I thought you told me you had to operate in the morning.

Harlan

You don't have to worry about me.

Grace

But I do.

Harlan

You're the one who needs rest now. You haven't been feeling too strong, you know.

Grace

Don't worry about me.
(*Harlan sits on the side of her bed*)
You know what I was thinking, Harlan?

Harlan

What?

Grace

That time when you graduated from the eighth grade, and your daddy took us on that lovely trip to Yellowstone Park? Remember that?

Harlan

(*Brushing aside other thoughts*) Yes. I remember.

Grace

The color of those mountains! And those giant trees! Do you remember what you said when you looked up at those trees for the first time?

Harlan

What?

Grace

You looked up and you said, "Gee, Mother—those trees must have been here a long time! Why, they must be older than Grandpa!"

Harlan

(*Smiling and shaking his head*) Did I say that?

Grace

That's what you said.

Harlan

(*Getting up*) Well, it is kind of late, Mother. I *do* have to operate in the morning and *you* have to get your rest.

Grace

(*Smiling*) Well, you're the doctor.

Harlan

Yes. Goodnight, Mother.
(*He turns to leave*)

Grace

Harlan?

Harlan

What?

Grace

I know you were with Susan tonight. And I couldn't help thinking that sooner or later you're going to have to make a decision. I know it's selfish of me, but I can't help hoping that we can have just a little more time together.

Harlan

Don't think about all that now, Mother. We'll talk about it tomorrow. Goodnight.

Grace

Goodnight, dear.
(*Closeup of Harlan as he closes the door of his mother's room. His face is weary and perplexed*)

Older than Grandpa!

I arrived home feeling a little older than Grandpa myself.

"Wasn't that scene today the same one you played last week?" Angela said as we sat down to dinner.

"No, no!" I growled irritably, cutting hard into a slice of veal and sending it off the plate. "This week I was 'weary and perplexed,' last week I was 'grim and pensive.' Can't you keep up?"

"Don't forget little Tommy's father Sunday," said Angela.

"Little Tommy's father Sunday? What is that, a riddle?"

"Chris's little friend, Tommy," clarified Angela. "Little Tommy's father is a fan of yours, remember? He wants to meet you. I told you on the phone, remember?"

"Oh," I managed.

"You're supposed to play softball with him on Sunday. He plays every Sunday."

"Oh, God!"

"Diamond six."

"God!"

"Chris and Tommy are very excited," Angela added.

"Little Tommy's father is a fan?" I said.

"Of course!"

"I don't know," I said after a decent pause.

"Tommy is Chris's best friend," emphasized Angela.

"I know, I know," I said.

"Don't be grouchy," soothed Angela.

With my 1950 Lonnie Frey model mitt tucked under my arm and Chris skipping excitedly at my side, we headed for diamond six on Sunday.

Tommy's father greeted us. Early forties—hair springing up and out over the neck of his tee shirt—baseball pants, spikes, muscular arms, five o'clock shadow—

"Hi ya doin', doc. Great meetin' ya!" he said, grabbing me. "I'm Tommy's father—a fan a' yours."

"Nice to meet you," I said, extracting my hand and punching it into my Lonnie Frey special, right through the busted webbing.

"This is a real kick meeting you, you know that," he continued, grinning. "I work nights, see, and the little woman got me hooked on your show, know what I mean? So when Tommy says that Chris's old man is on the show, I scream 'Holy cow!' know what I mean? 'I know dat guy!'

Right? Dr. Cross—sure. See him every day. Hey, guys! here's Dr. Cross—Harlan, right?"

"Yeah. Hi," I said, waving.

All the guys were wearing spikes and caps and muscles like Tommy's father. Zipping the ball around the infield, shouting, grim faced.

"Ha!"

"Ya!"

"Roun' na horn!"

"Yo!"

"Wa!"

Tommy's father had his hand up under his tee shirt, punching his stomach with a closed fist. "We play in a league out on the Island on Thursdays, come in here on Sunday—keep in shape, ya know?" (Whack!)

"Ya!"

"Ha!"

The stands were filled with old guys sitting on newspapers and smoking cigars. Chris and Tommy took front-row seats.

"Lefty, huh?" says Tommy's father, rolling a ball down his arm, popping it off his bicep, catching it backwards. Chris and Tommy cheered. I was staring down at my Lonnie Frey special.

"Didn't know there was any left-handed surgeons, ha, ha!"

"Ha ha."

"How about right field?" suggests Tommy's father.

"All right," I said.

"If the ball hits the tree, it's all you can get," he explains.

(Sudden vision: first pitch of the game—wicked line drive right off the tree hitting me in the kisser, guy running all the way around. Chris and Tommy booing.)

"Right field's fine," I said.

Third inning. I'm standing out in right field, next to the tree. No score. Two on, two out. Left-handed hitter—about 6′ 3″ (Jesus, look at the shoulders!) Whack! Son of a bitch! I'm running to my right—stick out the old Lonnie Frey—THWACK! Got it! Out!

"Ha!"

"Wa!"

"Way ta go!"

Crowd cheering. Chris and Tommy yelling.

"Nice going, Dad!"

Fifth inning. No score. I come up to the plate.

"This guy's easy!" yells the catcher, an ugly guy with a face like the bottom of a foot. Body shaped like a clock.

"Let's get the doc with the glasses!" he yells, grinning crookedly. "I got this pop up!" A real loudmouth.

"You're gonna die right dere, doc!"

(Up yours, foot face.)

"Hit it, Dad!" Chris yelled from the stands.

THWACK! Hoy boy! Line drive—off the tree! Go! Go! Rounding second—the ball bobbled—all you can get! Keep going! Score! I'm running like hell for the plate— throw comes in—foot face is hunched there, catching it, blocking the plate. Slide! Hit it! I hurled myself at him, feet high. CRUNCH! Foot face is groaning and holding the ball up—and I'm on top of him. The lights were going out.

I came to, lying in the grass behind the stands. A young fellow in a blue suit saying he was a med student—grabbing at my ankle. Chris and Tommy peering down at me.

"I think you might have a broken ankle." The med student has his jacket off. Change is spilling out of his pocket.

"Broken?" I say, picking change out of the grass and holding it out to him.

A cop car appears. Tommy's father is helping me into the back seat.

"Gee, I'm sorry, doc—hope you're OK! Sure was nice ta meet ya."

Sirens blaring.

Angela, in a state of shock, called Dr. Guilbert.

"Oh, Steven—your ankle—so swollen!"

"I was sliding home," I said.

Poor Angela, who asks me what inning it is when I'm

watching football on TV, is trying to figure it out. Slide? Home?

"What?" she said.

"Playing with little Tommy's father who's a fan," I said.

"My God, Steven, you have to do the show tomorrow!"

Dr. Guilbert arrived. "Looks like a possible fracture. I'll have to get some X rays. Let's go."

In the taxi to Dr. Guilbert's office, I stared down at my ankle. It looked like a good-sized Indian River grapefruit.

He was right. A fracture.

"You'll be in this cast for at least two weeks," he said. "Be a week before you can stand on it."

I looked terrific, silhouetted in the doorway of our apartment on my new crutches, pants leg cut to the thigh, cast from toe to knee. Angela gave a cry.

Stretched out on the bed, I riffled urgently through the pages of the next day's script.

"Oh, my God!"

"What is it?" whispered Angela.

"I've got an operation in Act I and a love scene with Susan in Act III. I'm supposed to pursue her around the apartment!"

"Oh, Steven!"

"*Now* they have me pursuing her! Call Hal," I said.

He wasn't in.

Meanwhile I memorized the two scenes, trying to imagine how I was going to manage them on one leg.

We finally got Hal.

"Hello, Hal? It's Steven."

"Steve, babe!"

"Hal, I've fractured my ankle. I'll be there tomorrow, but the doctor says I won't be able to get around on it for about a week. I'll need a wheelchair. Are you there, Hal?"

"Who is this? Come on!" Hal said. "Is this Danny? Who is this? Max?"

"It's no joke, Hal. This is Steven—I'm not kidding."

(Long pause.)

"I'm putting the phone over my heart now, Steven. Can you hear that?"

"I'm sorry, Hal."

"No sound, notice? It's stopped beating."

"Look, I'll *be* there, Hal—don't worry."

"*I'm* not worrying. It's my heart, Steven. You should see the expression it's wearing. It's stopped completely. Hear that?"

"I'll see you tomorrow, Hal."

My leg, throbbing angrily during the night, kept waking me up with loud, hostile thumps. The next morning, Angela, fussing sweetly, helped me get ready and out the door.

Getting into my morning taxi was like going through the rolling barrel in the fun house. My arm wrapped around our doorman, Angela opening the taxi door in the rain, crutch dropping in a large puddle.

My cab driver was a finicky type. He had all these handpainted signs in the back of the cab:

PLEASE DO NOT SMOKE—I AM ASTHMATIC
PLEASE DO NOT PUT FEET ON JUMP SEATS
DO NOT THROW THINGS ON FLOOR

"My first call a' the day, and I get someone with a bum leg!" he whined, swiping feverishly at the windshield with a man-sized Kleenex.

"I'm sorry," I said. "Didn't mean to depress you."

"Last week I had a cripple in here, screwed off part of his leg and left it in the cab. Imagine that? Lotta nuts in this town, boy! Hey, watch that crutch, would ya! That's new upolstery, you know."

"It's not on the upolstery," I said, trying not to imagine the missing leg man, staggering around the curb—waving, yelling.

"I suppose your feet are all wet back there, huh?"

At the front of the studio were Hal and Tom Curtis, waiting to help me inside. The driver ran around supervising my withdrawal from his Better Homes and Gardens taxicab.

"Watch the paint on a' door dere!"

Hal held an umbrella over our heads as Tom grabbed

at me. I leaned heavily on him and we lurched into the lobby.

"Wait a minute! Oh!" grunted Tom.

"What's up?" said Hal, running over and grabbing me.

"My back!" groaned Tom. "I think something popped. Did you hear a pop?" He leaned forward painfully. Inside the lobby door was my wheelchair. Hal helped me into it and began pushing me toward the elevator—Tom leaning heavily on one of my crutches and moaning quietly. We made our way to the studio.

Small craft warnings were up at the studio, all systems go—to see if I could be got through the day. Max, madly plotting alternate sets of camera shots. Hal was on the phone long distance with the writers about possible script alterations. Terry and the casting director were conferring about finding a stand in for certain shots, or worse, a replacement in case things became impossible.

(Sudden image: a battalion of tall, blond, two-legged actors—rushed over from central casting, wandering around the building looking for Multipurpose Room 3.)

In my distraction, I had managed for the first time to forget my locker key. Kate, reeling from the double horror of seeing me in my spiffy aluminum wheelchair and hearing that I'd forgotten the key, raced down the hall, arms flapping, looking for someone strong to break open my locker. I imagined Willy blasting the lock off with his gun.

How to tackle my operation in Act I came in for trials and errors right up to the air show. Harlan had to remove the gall bladder of a close personal friend of Dr. Nevins. Nevins, on one of his infrequent returns to the table, was to assist. (Gustav in his green mask and cap looking like a large forest creature.)

By dress rehearsal, Max had arrived at having me propped on one leg up against the operating table, and having Frank, a broadbacked stagehand, kneeling under the table supporting my good leg and holding me in place.

"Think you can manage on one leg like that if Frank holds you?" asked Max.

"I think so," I said.

Frank crawled under the table. Court helped get my leg over the shoulder.

"I got'cha, kid!" whispered Frank, as still as death under the table. Nurses were anxiously waiting Court's cue to start doing things, handing me the hardware as Dr. Nevins and I conferred in hushed voices, interposed with my instrument commands.

"Looks like the right lobe."

"Yes. Scalpel."

"Difficult—those hepatic veins."

"Sponge."

"Small tumor in the biliary tract."

"Drainage tube ready?"

"Yes, doctor."

Cutting and peering intently, I became conscious of a sudden tom-tom throb in my good leg—the one with the funny knee on it—pulsing, beating, cramping. I could feel Frank's broad back beginning to quiver sympathetically.

"Obstructed jejunum."

"What do you think, doctor?" (Frank groaning under the table now.)

"Suture."

"Yes, doctor."

"Fundus." (The cramp was gaining voltage—gripping, roaring.)

"Insert tube."

"Distensible walls." (The pain was shooting up through my good left calf, pausing, resting, then up toward—my knee.)

"Epithelium."

"Clamp!" I yelled, falling straight down under the table. A shower of instruments clattered to the floor. Frank grunted and began crawling away. The nurses scattered. Gustav fell on his knees in cap and mask, looking like a wounded elf, then struggled to help Court lift me up.

Max came running out on the floor, followed by Hal racing over with the wheelchair.

"You all right, babe?"

"Slipped," I said.

"We'll have to try something else for air," said Max, his voice deadened with deliberate calm.

The Act III love scene in Susan's apartment was even trickier. At last, Harlan was to take action. The scene began with Susan sulking about Harlan's putting off the engagement. Harlan must go to her and try to put his arms around her. She pushes him away and rushes into the bedroom, locking the door. Angrily, Harlan demands that she open the door. She refuses. Furious now, he smashes his shoulder against the door, breaking the lock, grabs her—the two of them falling onto the bed. Then he must hold her in a passionate embrace at the fade.

The kind of scene I'd been waiting for. Some action! And here I was being wheeled around the studio like a wizened invalid!

The use of a double was finally settled upon. A guy looking enough like me to be able to do the moves. Max had devised an intricate set of cuts. For example, my double would move toward Susan on the couch. Then Max would cut to Susan, during which I would hop onto the couch and grab her for the "two-shot" (the two of us on the couch). Later the guy would bust down the door and run at her. Closeup of Susan lying back on the bed looking appalled. Then he would duck down out of sight while I hobbled out from behind the door and crawled toward her along the bed.

Cynthia Lewis, our casting director, remembered seeing a guy in a cigarette commercial who looked exactly like me. She called the agency which handled the account, and somehow located him and had him in the studio at noon.

He looked like me all right. But how to get him to race across the room like me was something else again.

He was wearing an orange blouse, with a scarf the size of a tablecloth tied around his throat, blue sunglasses, and a tan the color of fried chicken.

"Hi, I'm Bruce," he said.

"How are ya," I said, reaching up out of my wheelchair.

"Awfully sorry about the ankle," said Bruce. "Poor you!"

"This is Jennifer," I said.

"Are you the one?" said Bruce.

"That's me," said Jennifer.

"You're a beauty! Where'd you get that skirt?"

Max had come over, ready to start working out the routine.

"Are you Bruce?"

"Right, yes. You want to start, don't you? I can see that," said Bruce, sinking down onto the couch, the sleeves of his orange blouse ballooning after him like toy parachutes.

Earlier in the day, before the advent of Bruce, we had tried having me wheel around to different encounter spots, throwing my voice, standing up in the chair for close head shots and various other fakeries that had the cameramen busting up and Max making his swan noises over the P.A.

Now we had Bruce racing across the room at Susan, the cut to Susan, then me popping up in his place on the couch as Bruce ducked out of frame, waiting for his next bit: busting down the door.

"Let's try it again," suggested Max, "a little less graceful this time, OK, Bruce?"

Bruce tried it again, Ice Capading across the room in his orange blouse, then swooning, frondlike, out of sight behind the couch.

"Now listen, Susan," I said, panting up out of nowhere beside her, trailing my plaster leg like a log on a string. "We've got to be patient. This is a difficult time!" I said, my left arm groping around her shoulder.

"NO!" said Susan, pushing my arm away, fighting tears. "I'm tired of being patient, Harlan!" Then breaking away from me and heading for the bedroom, opening the door, and disappearing inside with an angry click of the lock.

"Susan, listen to me," I continued into the boom mike over the sofa. "Come here, Susan!"

"Cue Bruce!" I could hear Max's swan yell right through Court's headset.

Bruce rising phoenix-like from behind the sofa and swooshing to the door. Closeup: his hand on the doorknob.

"Open this door, Susan!" I yelled.

Bruce rattling the doorknob. Closeup of Bruce's shoulder. Bruce's shoulder smashing against the door and the door not giving. Bruce bouncing backwards.

"Oh, Mary!" he yelled, grabbing at himself, his face contorting.

Max was shouting over the P.A. "What's the matter with that door? It's supposed to pop open!"

Two grips with screwdrivers and hammers shuffled onto the set.

"You OK, Bruce?"

No answer from Bruce as he examined himself grimly.

"Try the other shoulder. Get that door fixed—we're losing time!" Max's voice was swelling urgently. "Take it from Susan's move out of the room."

"This is crazy!" muttered Jennifer, coming back to the couch and sitting down.

"It'll work! It'll work!" Max's voice vibrated with promise over the P.A.

We started again.

"Susan, listen to me! Come here, Susan!"

Bruce's other shoulder smashed through the door this time. Closeup of Susan recoiling on the bed. Court helping me through the doorway. Bruce ducking out of sight again. Me crawling onto the foot of the bed toward Susan, then grabbing her. Very tight two-shot of our upper torsoes as I pin her in an embrace—a kiss—Susan giving way. Theme music. And fade out.

"It'll work!" repeated Max. "Do it just like that and we'll make it."

But what about the operation in Act I? How was that going to work? This had been dress rehearsal. In an hour I'd be on the air—hacking away at those bile ducts.

I lay on the set bed, my head still in Jennifer's lap.

"How ya doin'?" she asked solicitously.

At the other end of the studio, I could hear another scene being played. Dress rehearsal going on inexorably, like a river.

At the foot of the bed lay my leg, staring at me and throbbing furiously.

"Great," I said.

"Jees, I watched that operation—when you fell!"

"Wait till you see it next time," I said.

"Can I do anything?" asked Jennifer. "Your toes are all blue. Would you like a pill or something?"

"No thanks," I braved.

Hal came over.

"OK, babe? Come on, we'll get you down to your room."

I got back into the wheelchair—hunched down, head rolling back like something being shoved along the boardwalk.

"You better lie down for a while," continued Hal. "Max has an idea for the operation."

"You mean they're going to operate on me instead?"

"Ha, ha—not yet, babe. No, he's having the operating table cut down, lowered. Then you'll all be sitting around it instead of standing."

"Sitting around it?"

"Yeah, and he's going to shoot low so you'll *look* like you're standing while you're operating. Be a real first. Ha, ha! Go, babe!"

"*Sit* around the table and operate," I said, trying to imagine it.

"Right, babe. Max'll show you before the air show. I kind of liked it the other way, when you fell down on top of Frank, but Max didn't get the humor."

As we got to my dressing room Kate was chugging down the hall with twin sweater and slacks outfits for me and my double.

"You guys are going to look real cute in these," she said, throwing mine in my lap. "I want you to know I shopped an hour for them. Between getting your locker open and buying this stuff . . . where's Bruce?" And she was off.

Naomi came by after Hal had helped me deposit myself on the cot.

"You've got to get some rest, Steven," she said, wetting her handkerchief under the faucet and swabbing my face. "Try to get some sleep—just a quick nap. Here . . . ." She covered me with my coat, turned off the lights and quietly left the room.

A moment later a knock. It was Gustav.

"You all right, old cock?"

"Just resting," I said.

"Brought you a sip of brandy," he said, extending a Dixie cup.

"Thanks," I said.

"Nothing fancy, you understand, but the wine list is rotten in this place," he said, backing out of the room and closing the door gently.

Alone in the dark now, sipping brandy and asking my ankle to be quiet, I tried warding off disaster images: my asthmatic knee going berserk in the middle of the operation—knocking over the table—my gall bladder man rolling off into our laps. And later Bruce, lying in a heap of shattered collarbone. And me, of course, tripping over him on my way through the door—a wayward camera catching me thrashing around, waving my cast. Twelve million watchers incredulized. Switchboards jamming.

Ten minutes before air, Gustav and three nurses and I were seated on stools around the sawed-off operating table, practicing our instrument passing like people in a booth at a Chinese restaurant spearing at things with chopsticks. My cast was propped up under the table on two telephone books.

"I'll say grace and you carve," whispered Gustav, as Max lined up new shots—tight closeups of arms, hands, and faces.

"You all look too stiff," he complained.

"It feels so weird," I said. "It's a whole different leverage."

From a sitting position my elbows stuck out at odd new angles, and my hands seemed to grow out of my face, gripping the instruments ludicrously in my slippery surgical gloves.

"Relax your torsoes," urged Max.

"Jesus," I said, trying to relax my torso, squatting there with my leg on the Yellow Pages. We were all staring at each other over our face masks, our elbows pointed.

"One minute to air, folks." Court's voice sounded hollow and dreamlike. I stole a quick look under the table. Leg still there. I felt disembodied. Current flowing through me as if I'd just been plugged in like an electric appliance. Suddenly I noticed what a long nose the nurse across from me had. I imagined her as a kid trying to eat an ice cream cone. Gustav's eyebrows seemed drawn on graph paper. (Never mind all that! Concentrate, dummy! Concentrate!)

There was the white blur of Court's script.

"Looks like the right lobe."

(Hoy boy!)

"Yes. Scalpel." (Nurse with the nose passing scalpel under my chin. I grab at it, trying to relax my upper torso.)

"Hepatic veins." (Gustav's face mask ballooning with breath.)

"Sponge."

"Biliary tract."

"Drainage tube ready?"

The nurse on my left was trying to figure out how to present the drainage tube from a seated position. (Hadn't tried *that* bit.)

Long empty pause. (Come on, sweetheart—there's a rotten-looking bile duct here! Clocks are running. My leg is itching!)

"Tube!" I said.

"Yes, doctor," she said, faking it.

"Obstructed jejunum."

What was this? Gustav, peering into the white stomach, and probably nervous over the missing drainage tube, was starting to rise inadvertently out of his chair like a confused after-dinner speaker.

"What do you think, doctor?" I said, staring straight at Gustav's stomach. He made a funny gurgling sound and sank back down, stunned, his brows arched up around his scalp.

"Suture."

Her hands shaking violently, the nose girl was making clanking noises with the hardware.

An attack of nerves was coming on. You can feel it start. It gets in the air—everyone picking up the message at the same instant like hand holders at a seance. Next to me, the tube nurse dropped her head forward; her shoulders were quivering.

There was a terrible pause while I waited for the suture.

"Tube ready!" blurted the girl.

"Good," I said (Good?), reaching over for the suture with my torso relaxed and trying to stay in frame.

"Fundus" was next for Gustav, a word he'd had trouble with all day.

"Fungus," he said, staring sure-eyed at the gall man's whiteness.

(Fungus! Fungus in the biliary tract!)

I felt an implosion of nervous, hidden laughter—a grenade going off just inside my rib cage.

"Insert tube!" I barked.

But my tube girl was no more. Heaving and shaking pitiably, she had lost the use of hands and brain.

Elaborately, I pantomimed inserting the tube. Max would save us. Max would cut away from the table. Just head shots now. I could deal a bridge hand in there and the audience wouldn't know—make sandwiches, address letters.

"Clamp."

We were getting to the end now.

"Epithelium," said Gustav wisely.

(Good man! That's the stuff!)

"Well done, Dr. Cross."

"Thank you, doctor."

(Scene fading. Harlan continues working, but we know the crisis has past.)

Court waved his script.

One down and one to go.

"Good God!" sighed Gustav.

"How's your fungus?" I said, as Kate ran over to help me off with my surgeon's garb and on with my twin-for-a-day sweater and slacks outfit.

The suture nurse came over. There was a tear rolling down her nose at me.

"I'm awfully sorry, Mr. Prince . . . oh, excuse me."

Kate was pulling the voluminous green operating pants down over my hips.

"Forget it," I said. "We got all the fungus out anyway."

Gustav was gathering up the drainage tube girl and the three of them began moving quietly toward the door.

Act II was going on in the Paul and Nancy Markham dining room ten feet away: Stephanie and Alan finessing their way through a six-minute scene about lamb chops and driving to the country and whether to ask Ruth and Phil to come along.

Act III was coming up. Our Punch-and-Judy bit in Susan's apartment.

Jennifer sat waiting on the couch with the script in her lap, talking to herself. Bruce stood nearby, posing morosely like an angry mannequin in a Bonwit Teller window.

After dress rehearsal, Bruce, angrily massaging his upper arms, sent up some flak in Hal's office about how he didn't like what was happening to his shoulders, and how he didn't know—*really*—how he could do that door busting. Hal had to walk him around the room for ten minutes explaining how life was full of uncertainties, and how we all had to put our shoulders to the wheel—ha, ha, babe!

Kate, grunting and sweating, had to cut the inner seam of my slacks to get the right leg over the plaster cast.

"My God, Steven," she whispered frantically, "you should've known better, busting your ankle like that—playing around like a kid."

The ankle was screaming back at her—pulsing, ugly. My joints ached. I was conjuring headlines:

ACTOR COLLAPSES DURING TV SHOW
'WAS SLIDING INTO HOME' HE AVERS

"All right, come on!" hissed Kate, helping me into the chair and pushing me across the studio to Susan's apartment.

"Let's review those moves," I said as Jennifer rose to help me out of the chair.

Bruce was checking the door.

"If this Mary Ann door doesn't work, I'm going to sue!" he whispered, pouting.

We ran the cues: Bruce popping up, dashing madly, fluttering down; me, hopping into place. (Were we actually going to do this demented ballet in two minutes?)

"Steven?" Jennifer was looking at me strangely. "Your face is like all white right through the makeup!"

I shrugged bravely.

The cameras were coming around at us. Court hustled over from the Act II set. Stephanie, tremulous and apprehensive, came by to wish us luck. Jimmy was lining up his opening shot.

(No turning back now, fellas.)

"Mary, I'm nervous!" said Bruce, crouching down behind my chair.

We began.

Everything was going fine. Me hopping, Bruce swooping, Jennifer waiting. Max was right—it was working.

We whipped along to the climax of the scene.

"I'm tired of being patient, Harlan!" said Susan, moving toward the bedroom door, closing it behind her.

"Susan, listen to me! Come here, Susan," I said. Bruce hurled himself against the door with his left shoulder. An angry crunch. Nothing. The door was still solidly closed. Bruce turned toward me, his face a mask of fear and indecision.

"I said 'come here!'" I repeated, waving Bruce on wildly from the couch.

Court was crouched down under camera two, exhorting Bruce with clenched fists. Bruce bit his lips—tears welled angrily. He turned his back, aimed his *right* shoulder this time, and rushed madly again. The door crashed open. Bruce fell heavily, groaning and rolling under the bed.

(That's the way, Bruce, baby!)

Court maneuvered me quickly to the door. With a one-legged leap I fell onto the bed, dragged myself toward

Susan's huddled figure and rolled on top of her, grabbed her, embraced her—a long, angry, passionate kiss. Fade out.

While Court ministered to the bruised Bruce, Jennifer helped me out of the bed and into the wheelchair, pushing me out the studio door to the stair landing.

We began giggling now like two school kids after a terrible final exam, and finally managed to inch our way to my dressing room.

Inside, Jennifer fished around in her Gucci bag. She found two apples and a bag of peanuts.

"Forgot to eat lunch," she said, and we got to laughing again, uncontrollably.

I was throwing peanuts over my head and catching them in my mouth. Jennifer tried it and missed.

"Look at you," she said, "lying there with that ankle and everything and catching peanuts."

"There are probably a lot of guys who can catch peanuts with a cast on their leg," I said. "Maybe not in this country, but in Europe probably—in Greece. I'll bet there are a lot of Greeks who could do it."

"How do they break their ankles in Greece?" asked Jennifer.

"They get tangled up in fishing nets quite a lot."

We munched away at the apples and the peanuts—recalling the events of the day and exploding with fresh laughter at each one.

Gustav walked in with brandy and the report that Bruce was mad but only bruised.

"Fungus!" said Jennifer, and we were off again.

Soon the room began filling up: Naomi came by, Stephanie, Alan, Tom.

Tom quipped that the opening shot of the operation looked like a sit in.

"To demand healthier patients," suggested Gustav, distributing Dixie cups.

Hal and Max arrived.

"Steve, babe!"

"Someone get Bruce," I said.

"It worked, it worked," Max was saying as he sat in a corner sipping his brandy.

Naomi extended her cup toward me. "To a valorous performance," she said.

Bruce appeared in the doorway.

"For best performance by a shoulder," said Tom, handing Bruce a cup.

"Oh, heaven!" said Bruce.

"I didn't realize a fractured ankle could be so much fun!" said Hal. "What can we do tomorrow?"

"Maybe Tom could shatter his pelvis helping me back into a taxi," I offered, hopping toward the door and across the hall to call home.

"Angela?"

"Steven!" Angela's voice was high and keening.

"Look, I'm OK. I'm coming right home."

"I was worried."

"Did you like that bit where I busted open the door, huh?"

"How did you do all that?"

"Pretty good, huh?"

"You didn't do that! How could you? What about your ankle?"

"Don't worry, I've got it right here with me."

"How did you get around on that ankle?"

"That's nothing. You ought to see me catch peanuts."

"What?"

"I'm coming right home. Tell you all about it."

NINE

As I was off the show for the rest of the week anyway, the writers had time to conjure up a reasonable explanation for Harlan's limping return. Paul Markham and Dr. Nevins explained it to the world thusly:

Dr. Nevins
Paul, I'm afraid we will be somewhat shorthanded for a couple of weeks.

Paul
Oh?

Dr. Nevins
You haven't heard of Harlan's accident, then?

Paul
No.

Dr. Nevins
On his way home from the hospital yesterday, he came upon an accident on the highway, and as he was trying to minister to one of the victims, the car rolled back into him. Fractured his ankle.

Doctors don't fracture their ankles sliding into home plate. They're too busy saving people.

Dr. Guilbert had the cast off in time for my return, and with a cane I was able to get around pretty nicely. In another week I'd be able to try the old soft shoe.

As our last scene together (my famous leap and bedwards crawl) had ended on a note of crucial intimacy, it was obvious that Harlan and Susan had reached a crisis in their relationship. No turning back now. It was time for action. Clearly, words had been whispered after that fatal fade out. Promises exacted. Resolves panted urgently between the gasps and sighs.

Harlan's apartment—late at night. Harlan, returning, opens the door, still limping from his accident. He turns on the light. We see his face now: grim, urgent. We hear Grace's voice calling from her bedroom.

Grace

(*Off*) Harlan, is that you?

Harlan

Yes, Mother.

Grace

It's so late.

Harlan

(*Moving toward the door*) I know.

Grace

You know I worry, dear.

Harlan

Mother, I've got to talk to you.

Grace

Talk?

Harlan

Yes.

Grace

(*Sensing his mood, affects a breezy tone*) You look so serious, Harlan. That same look you used to have as a boy when you'd want to talk to me or Daddy about something that you *thought* was so important.

Harlan

Well, *this* is important all right.

Grace

(*Continuing her train of thought*) About school or some little problem that was on your mind, or some scheme or plan. So serious. Your face . . . .

Harlan

(*Interrupting*) Mother, listen to me. This isn't about school.

Grace

What *is* it about, Harlan?

Harlan

It's about Susan.

Grace

(*Her voice tightening*) Susan?

Harlan

And me.

Grace

Susan and you.

Harlan

Yes. We're getting married.

Grace

(*The words hit her like a blow, but she tries to remain calm*) I see. May I ask when?

Harlan

Next month.

Grace

(*She was not quite ready for this*) Next month!

Harlan

Yes.

Grace

But that's too soon! Where would we move to? What would . . . .

Harlan

(*Interrupting*) Aunt Cynthia has a big home in Santa

Barbara. She said once you'd be welcome to come out there and stay with her.

Grace

Aunt Cynthia? But she didn't mean . . . .

Harlan

I called her tonight. She said you can come anytime. Susan and I will take you out there, stay for a day or two and continue on to Hawaii.

Grace

Hawaii!

Harlan

That's where we're going for our honeymoon, Mother.

Grace

(*Dizzy from this succession of facts*) Well, you *did* have a scheme and a plan after all. My goodness, it's so much to comprehend all at once like this . . . .

Harlan

It's simple really.

Grace

Simple? (*Overcome with self-pity*) Oh, Harlan! (*She begins to cry—then to gasp for breath*) Harlan! (*She collapses back against her pillow, apparently unconscious*)

Harlan

(*Moving to the head of the bed, taking her hand. His voice concerned*)
Mother?
(*Fade Out*)

When the writers decide it's time for someone to see the light, or have a change of heart, they don't mess around. Attitudes that may have taken months or even a lifetime to accumulate and harden, determinations that have burned with a hard, gemlike flame, can be miraculously undone in a single stroke.

When Grace reluctantly recovered from her brief collapse, she awoke as from some dream—like an aging fairy queen: understanding, docile, selfless. She of the iron hand in a velvet glove, who had been holding on to Harlan with the tenacity of a tigress, was now cooing expectantly over the wedding and wondering about the tulips in Santa Barbara as if she were competing for the National Good Sport Award. I think if Harlan had informed her that she was being shipped off to Aunt Cynthia by Railway Express, she would have driven herself over to the post office for stamping.

"For Christ's sweet sake!" said Naomi at rehearsal. "All this amenable stuff all of a sudden! All this too too sweetie pie!"

Max offered his masonic smile. "Grace realizes she really wants what's best for her son. She sees that he really loves Susan. She finally has to admit to herself that Susan qualifies as a good wife. She realizes now that she's been fighting for something negative. She's trying to reverse that attitude."

"Uh huh," said Naomi. "You're sitting there with the pencils, Buster."

Max was looking at the clock. "Let's take it from Grace's line, 'Harlan, I was talking to Susan, and she agrees that the small chapel will be just perfect.' "

After rehearsal, Naomi and I walked slowly toward the makeup room together.

"Well," she said, "I'll see you in Santa Barbara."

"We're going to miss you," I said.

"I never thought I'd feel funny about this being over," she said. "But I do. It really *is* like a family here."

"I know," I said.

"When I'm back at the farm and puttering around in the garden some afternoon, I'll come back into the house, turn on the TV and I'll hear your voices. And there you'll be. You and Jennifer and Frances, Gustav, Stephanie, Tom—all of you."

We had reached the open door of the makeup room. Carl was standing by the chair.

"Would one of you two yo yo's mind getting your ass in this chair? I've got twelve people on the show today."

"You go ahead," said Naomi, "I'll start on my hair."

Pepe, who'd been napping on the couch, came to life. Naomi and I climbed into the chairs, catching each other's gaze in the mirror.

Celebrations are very popular on daytime serials. As in real life, they are the occasions for clan gathering. Christmas, New Year's, birthdays, deaths and weddings, those days when memories are stirred, and best wishes truly given.

If, with luck, Christmas falls on a weekday, there are carols sung and presents under the Markham tree. Phil Markham says grace before the big turkey dinner.

Funerals allow all the favorites to gather under one roof. And sprinkled among the regulars as the camera pans across the bereaved rows are a few old familiar faces come back to pay their respects.

Anniversaries, too, are very big. When Ruth and Phil Markham celebrated their twentieth wedding anniversary on the show Frances and Bill received over ten thousand letters and cards of congratulation.

But nothing beats a wedding. And Harlan's and Susan's wedding was given the full treatment.

Not only was there the event itself, but it was also Naomi's last day on the show. Spirits ran high—a special tension which you could see in looks and postures. There was a buzz, a quickening.

Aaron Rothman, our set designer, had created a beautiful nineteenth-century church interior: stained glass, rows of rich wooden pews, alabaster statuary—even a baptismal font set on one side. And a handsome reception room which Ross Manning, our set decorator, had filled with lavish silver and flowers and fine crystal.

Aaron, usually cucumber cool, was running around nervously giving directions to Ross and the stagehands.

"I guess we'd better tone down the mosaic tiling behind the nave—we don't want to clash with the bride." Frank, the broadbacked stagehand, trundled into the sanctuary area to soap down the tiles.

"I think we could use some pink upstage. How about dahlias, Ross?"

Getting ready for dress rehearsal, Gustav and I stood

in front of the mirror in my dressing room adjusting our striped ties and appraising each other, resplendent in morning coats.

"Well, old cock, you are a marvelous-looking groom," he said, struggling manfully with a too tight collar. "But your best man doesn't seem able to button a damn thing properly. Collar buttons and septic tanks . . . . " And he was gone in search of Kate.

I adjusted my boutonniere and began practicing a limpless walk around the room. There was a light knock on the door.

Jennifer.

In a flowing white gown with a filmy veil, and holding a bouquet of white narcissus, she stood in the doorway, a bride out of the storied past—a vision. She moved toward me and stood by my side. We faced the mirror together.

("Do you, Harlan Cross, take this woman . . . . ")

Was this Jennifer? The kooky girl leaning backwards and waving crazily from the red sports car? Jennifer? Cool and groovy?

("And do you, Susan Williams, take this man . . . . ")

That girl taking my arm in the mirror. Susan. And Harlan.

"You look beautiful," I said.

("In sickness and in health, for richer or poorer . . . . ")

After all those months! The waiting!

Harlan. Good fellow.

And Susan.

Susan looked up at me.

"You look beautiful," she murmured.

"The groom's not supposed to see the bride before the ceremony," I said.

She smiled and moved away toward the door, waving a small wave—the one I'd taught her—and then she glided out.

I looked back at the mirror.

Harlan!

The opening shot was a sideways view of the park by the church set, where, through the trees, you could see the lovely white vaulted entrance of the church. And standing on the steps, the distant figures of Frances and Bill, Tom, Stephanie and Alan—chatting, then entering. Then the rear of the church—people filing in and being ushered to their seats.

Gustav and I waited behind the sanctuary door for our cue, Gustav fiddling nervously with his tie and collar button.

"Got the ring?" I whispered.

Gustav slapped at his pocket. "Yes, yes," he said.

I was feeling shaky-kneed, wondering if I would get the vows right.

Court ducked his head around the corner.

"Go, baby!" he said.

Gustav propelled himself through the door. I followed. Ralph was playing the organ—rich, vibrant chords filled the room. We stood at the side, waiting—Gustav slapping at his jacket pocket again.

Besides all the regulars there was a large complement of extras, and, in the third row, Kate—dressed to the nines and beaming around. (Kate hasn't missed a trial or a wedding or a funeral in fifteen years.)

Closeup of Naomi in the first row wearing an indescribable hat from which her famous innerspring curls sprouted. Next to her a graying Rockwell Kent lady meant to be Susan's New England mother. And in the back, Susan's palsied aunt, who rode in on my aluminum wheelchair and sat now, shaking slightly and managing a few nods and smiles.

Ralph skillfully switched gears into the familiar bride's entrance theme. Heads turned. And there, on the arm of a tall, distinguished gentleman meant to be her father, came Susan. My Susan. Veiled, breathtaking—coming toward us. Gustav slapped at his pocket again and made a small sound.

We shuffled expertly into place.

"We are gathered here . . . ."

My thoughts spun backwards, sideways, then forward, and back again.

"I, Harlan, take this woman . . . . " It was a strange voice, sounding far away—someone else's voice.

Gustav was struggling with the ring.

"I do," whispered Jennifer.

I lifted her veil, and she looked up at me with glowing eyes. As I kissed her it seemed as if I were standing outside myself, watching, listening. I would gather Steven Prince up later and take him home. Meanwhile . . . .

Meanwhile, nobody could have had a more impressive wedding.

As Jennifer and I walked up the aisle, Kate was crying. So was Naomi. And the palsied aunt. There were rice throwers at the door. And when the scene faded, and Court waved his script and said, "Thanks, everybody," we all stood in place a little dimly for a minute, looking sheepish, then realizing there was another act to go.

There was a farewell party for Naomi after the show in the reception room set. Real champagne to fill the crystal glasses and a cake with "To Naomi With Love" written on it.

Hal was helping to draw the strange day to a close.

"OK, everybody! OK, gang!" He was popping his glass with a cake fork.

"Those glasses cost six dollars apiece," said Ross Manning sideways to Hal.

"OK, look—I'll rub my finger around the top. How's that?" said Hal. "Hey, people, I'm rubbing my finger around the top of my six-dollar glass to get your attention here!"

"This is a toast to Naomi: a lady who has captured our hearts and stolen our scenes and run off with the honors. In other words, she's a thief."

(Laughter.)

"Besides being a thief, she's a wonderful actress and a great person."

(Cheers.)

"We're going to miss her very much, and hope we can get her back with us again."

(Yes! Yes!)

"If Naomi will forgive me for saying this—when I was a boy, I fell in love with her in a dark movie theater in Findlay, Ohio. I fell in love with her then, and I'm still in love with her now. And I know you all feel that way too. Nami, babe, like it says on the cake, we love you!"

(Applause.)

"And as a small token of our affection . . . ."

Hal presented Naomi with a beautiful leather script binder with her initials on it.

Naomi, with a small catch in her voice, thanked Hal and everybody, and said how much she'd enjoyed working with us and being with us.

"And thank you especially for putting up with me in those first days. I love you too," she said.

We all stood in our wedding finery—the banks of lights over our heads, cameras and boom mikes standing silently by—saying goodby to Naomi and to the character she had played. Toasting with the same champagne glasses we had toasted with on the show. I kept expecting Max to holler a note out over the P.A.

("Steven, when you hand Naomi the cake, move farther downstage.")

But all this was really happening. Another person come and gone—another ending as prelude to some new beginning. The "logic of the circle," Bill Sievers had called it. "The final and inexorable balance and harmony—the continuum." Bill and his Hindu mandala.

I thought back to Naomi's first day. The excitement. And afterwards the calls pouring out over those phones. "Naomi, we love you."

And now she was going back to the farm.

"I'll be walking back through the house from the garden, and I'll hear your voices," she'd said.

The party was breaking up.

"I'll come by one day and see you," Naomi kept saying.

Jennifer seemed reluctant to leave. She moved about dreamily, drinking champagne and catching images of herself in the soaped-down mirror over the liquor table.

"For God's sake, get out of that gown, will ya?" said

Kate. "Steven, get your bride out a' here before she ruins that dress."

Gustav had his arm around Naomi. "Well, Naomi, my sweetheart, we see each other again soon, yes? We'll have you out to our place sometime when the septic tank is not overflowing."

"Oh, I'll come by one day anyway," said Naomi.

It was definitely time to go.

"So long, pal," I said, taking Naomi's hand and kissing her. "We'll see each other."

"I'll come around and see you all," she repeated. We were both smiling cheerily. There was a pause.

"Right," I said.

I moved slowly away and out of the studio toward my room. There were running steps behind me.

"Wait up!" said Jennifer, running to me and taking my hands. "Well, we're married," she said softly. She still carried the white bouquet, ribboned and beginning to wilt around the edges after the long day.

I walked her to her room.

"Be careful with that dress," I said. "Kate'll have a fit."

"Yes," she murmured.

There were a few leftover specks of rice in her hair. I brushed them away.

"Rice," I said.

"Oh."

"Well."

"Yes?"

"See you."

"See you," said Jennifer.

I walked to my room and undressed slowly. My ankle felt a little stiff.

When I got home, the doorman handed me a package of scripts for the following week. No one was home. Charley barked effusively, as he does when he's been left alone.

I fed the fish and sprawled out on the couch with my scripts. What kind of honeymoon were we going to have? How was I going to respond to my new married life?

Act I

Fade In:
Hawaii. A luau at Queen's Surf on Waikiki Beach. It is
night. Torches light the palm trees swaying in the breeze.
(Note: This sequence will be shot at Jones Beach on Sun-
day, August 24.) Harlan and Susan, wearing Picaci leis,
have finished eating. They are drinking rum punch out of
pineapple shells. A Hawaiian band is playing. There is a
full moon. On the sand a row of native girls are performing
a sensual Tahitian hula.

Susan
(Smelling the flowers of her lei) Smell these flowers,
Harlan—aren't they beautiful!

Harlan
(Smelling the flowers) Yeah, great.

Susan
What a lovely night. Look at those stars!
(But Harlan is mesmerized now by the Tahitian dancers)

Harlan
Yes, dear.

Susan
The Big Dipper! Look, Harlan!

(Closeup: Girls gyrating intensely to the wild beat of the
drums. Then a closeup of Harlan staring at them, riveted.
Slowly, he begins to smile—the old knifelike grin)

Susan
(Oblivious) Harlan! Look at that moon!